"The first ant arrived just as he finished making the capsule safe. He could see it clearly through the transparent side of the container and to Dilke it seemed as big as a pony. He crouched fearfully as it ran its twitching antennae over the capsule and bit at the curved surface with its massive toothed jaws. Then Dilke was surrounded by ants, their dark blood-red armor gleaming, their articulated legs rattling together as they scrambled around and over the capsule. It rocked and rolled violently, throwing Dilke from side to side. The container's smooth, pliable and slightly soapy surface defeated all their efforts to get at the creature inside. They hoisted it up and started back the way they had come....

"....Dilke felt the walls of the capsule turn cold and wet with condensation; he wiped it away and as his eyes became accustomed to the gloom he realized that he was being carried down a long sloping tunnel, deep into the earth. A soft, bluish light lit the passage, and when at last it widened, the phosphorescent glow illuminated a vast open chamber. Its floor was thronged with ants, its walls and arched roof were covered with a cellular pattern alive with ants. He was in a City of Ants."

COLD WAR IN A
was originally publis
G. P. Putnam's Sons.

D0926329

Lindsay Gutteridge

COLD WAR
IN A
COUNTRY
GARDEN

PUBLISHED BY POCKET BOOKS NEW YORK

COLD WAR IN A COUNTRY GARDEN

Putnam edition published July, 1971

POCKET BOOK edition published February, 1973

This POCKET BOOK edition includes every word
contained in the original, higher-priced edition. It is printed
from brand-new plates made from completely reset, clear, easy-to-read
type. POCKET BOOK editions are published by POCKET BOOKS, a division
of Simon & Schuster, Inc., 630 Fifth Avenue, New York, N.Y. 10020.
Trademarks registered in the United States and other countries.

L

To Annie and to Richard

And now to the Abbyss I pass
Of that unfathomable Grass,
Where men like Grashoppers appear,
But Grashoppers are Gyants there:
They, in their squeaking Laugh, contemn
Us as we walk more low then them:
And, from the Precipices tall
Of the green spir's, to us do call.

(Andrew Marvell)

PART ONE

1

Mathew Dilke stood in the June sun and looked up at his rockery. The sun had burned his forehead and shoulders a bright pink; the rest of his naked body had the pallor of a mill-worker on a day trip to the sea.

He was a strongly built man, like an all-in wrestler, with bunchy shoulders and a short neck; agile in spite of a thick waist.

Age: thirty-seven.

Hair: receding.

His most dramatic feature: a nose like a scimitar jutting out of a broad face, very thin with flared nostrils. It gave his face a touch of nervous arrogance.

The little alpines had rooted well since he had planted them in the spring, the pink flowerettes on the London Pride had turned white and were falling like confetti.

The lawn needed mowing; in his absence it had got out of hand. He strolled along the base of the rockery towards the western end where the hollyhocks grew; as he looked up he saw a movement on a leaf. An ant which had been rapidly moving along the leaf edge suddenly stopped; two other ants appeared beside the first motionless insect. Dilke felt uneasy, the creatures seemed to be observing him; he decided to move away, and as he did so the leaf swung and tilted slightly with the weight of more ants which appeared on its edge. As if on command they turned, ran to where the leaf joined the main stem of the plant and started to descend its thick stalk. Dilke looked up at the vast broken slopes of the rockery, tracing with his eyes a route through its maze of cliff-like rocks and steep slopes.

He took the first slope at a hard run, his impetus carrying him up to the first rock. He caught the trailing strands of a crawling rock plant and pulled himself up the stone face.

He ran and climbed steadily towards the summit where the rockery met the lawn, his feet loosened the soil, tumbling it down the slopes in small avalanches. Climbing on to the topmost rock he sat for a moment to regain his breath. Far below him he saw the ants running in line, coming very fast.

They were about thirty minutes behind him. He got to his feet and turned and ran into the lawn. Daisies grew profusely and he ran through the forest of their stalks, their heads forming an almost continuous canopy above him; the sunlight filtered down through the white petals throwing a luminous light over the green moss on which he travelled.

He came to the first crazy-paving stone and climbed up on to it. Now that he had left the shelter of the lawn a hard, dry wind struck him, making his patches of sunburn smart. He looked back towards the rockery, searching for his pursuers, but nothing moved except the tossing sea of daisy heads. He turned and looked along the paved pathway that led to the compost bin behind the laurels. The paving stretched before him, each stone separated from its neighbour by a shallow valley. He set off at a fast jog, the smooth stone surface bouncing the sunlight up into his squinting eyes.

Down into the first valley; up on to the second stone with a glance back for the ants.

Down into the second valley; glance back.

Third valley; as he plunged down its side he disturbed a Cabbage White which was sunbathing out of the breeze. It went up like a mad helicopter, the wind from its huge powdery wings tossing the grass blades, and Dilke slipped and fell among a shower of dislodged wing scales; a crosswind caught the butterfly and carried it out of sight over the valley edge.

When he climbed on to stone number three and looked back, the first of the ants were leaping into view. They

streamed on to the first paving stone, travelling more
quickly than Dilke, but he stuck to his even jog. When
he ran on to the last of the crazy-paving slabs, they were
only one stone behind him. He increased his speed and
when he came to the sloping ground which lay in the
shadow of the laurels he sprinted between the hills of
trash which had spilled from the compost bin; across
potato peelings, round squashed lemons, and amongst a
litter of broken eggshells he found the drug capsule. It
lay in two halves, one half filled by a drop of water. He
emptied it and stepped in, pulling the second half over his
head, tugging and twisting to make a tight friction fit. The
moulded edges were imperfectly finished and sufficiently
rough to give him hand-holds. Assembled, it was almost
three-eighths of an inch long, giving ample room to move
and breathe.*

The first ant arrived just as he finished making the
capsule safe. He could see it clearly through the transparent side of the container and to Dilke it seemed as
big as a pony. He crouched fearfully as it ran its twitching antennae over the capsule and bit at the curved surface with its massive toothed jaws. Then Dilke was surrounded by ants, their dark blood-red armour gleaming,
their articulated legs rattling together as they scrambled
around and over the capsule. It rocked and rolled violently, throwing Dilke from side to side. The container's
smooth, pliable and slightly soapy surface defeated all
their efforts to get at the creature inside. They hoisted it
up and started back the way they had come. Then instead
of carrying him north along the paved way they struck
off to the west on a trail through the lawn.

At first the trail was deserted, but Dilke saw from the
interior of his jerking vehicle that more and more ants
were using the track, until at last they joined a main
thoroughfare. Here the ants travelled in both directions;
those going the same way as Dilke's captors were
burdened with loot: leaves, sticks, pieces from the car-
cases of larger insects, living green aphids. Those going
the other way were unencumbered, travelling at a run.

Suddenly they went from the glaring sunlight into dark-

---

* Dilke stands below Marvell—page vii.

ness. Dilke felt the walls of the capsule turn cold and wet with condensation, he wiped it away and as his eyes became accustomed to the gloom he realized that he was being carried down a long sloping tunnel, deep into the earth. A soft, bluish light lit the passage and, when at last it widened, the phosphorescent glow illuminated a vast open chamber. Its floor was thronged with ants, its walls and arched roof were covered with a cellular pattern, alive with ants. He was in a City of Ants.

His presence in the capsule stirred the ants near him into a frenzy of excitement and they tried to break through the wall to attack him. He was thrown dizzily about inside the capsule but once more the ants were unable to break in. When they gave up their attempts the capsule had rolled into a short cul-de-sac which branched off a passage leading from the City Hall. As the hours passed cold struck through the walls of the capsule and Dilke shifted his bruised limbs restlessly to keep warm. His thoughts, fixed on his desolate future, were interrupted by the sounds of shuffling feet on the floor of the passageway and the scraping of insect bodies pushing along its walls. He sat up and rubbed away the mist on the inside of the capsule with his forearm. Passing the end of the cul-de-sac was a herd of green aphids; they trudged stolidly along, herded by a small number of ant workers. When the aphid cows came to a stop, the ants moved amongst them delicately milking them of their honey dew, gently stroking the cows with their feelers and eagerly licking up the drops of fluid. The milkers went after a while leaving the aphids crowded in the passageway, a few of them wandered into the dead-end passage and stood near Dilke's capsule. After some hesitation and encouraged by his growing hunger, Dilke forced open the capsule and stepped out.

It was bitterly cold. There was a strange mixture of smells on the air, part chemical, part decayed flesh and part the sickly sweet smell of aphid milk. The creatures appeared to be docile and not alarmed by Dilke; they came waist-high and he walked quietly amongst them, mimicking the actions of the ants, and was rewarded by gifts of the sweet excreta. Its flavour, though unlike anything Dilke had ever tasted, was not unpleasant. It filled his belly and he returned satisfied to his refuge.

Two things had impressed Mathew Dilke about this micro-world: the high wind which prevailed above ground, and the noise underground. It was like an underwater recording of marine life which he had once heard: groans, roars, clicks, throbbing bumping sounds; combined with a high-pitched fluctuating noise like electronic sound-waves.

The subterranean life gave few indications of the passing of time, but Dilke thought he detected a pattern of activity. The aphid herds came and went, the ants surged like city workers back and forth along the passageway, the volume of noise rose and fell.

There was no future for Dilke in this byeway in an ants' nest.

He waited till the noise of insect traffic died down and when the pipings and clickings had stopped he opened the capsule and crept to the main passage. It was deserted. From his right came a humming sound, to his left the tunnel sloped upwards. He walked to the left slowly and fearfully now that he was without protection. He had entered a labyrinth of tunnels and he decided always to take the route which led upwards. After an hour of slow progress the light grew fainter and fainter until he could see nothing before him. The ground beneath his feet became rough and littered with stones and he could no longer feel the walls with his hands.

Dilke felt utterly weary. The stress of his experiences, his inadequate diet, and now the feeling of being entombed without light and without hope of escape, crushed his spirits. He closed his eyes against the blackness, his head fell back, his arms hung loosely at his sides. After a while he opened his eyes; above his head he saw the winking lights of the Plough and low down on the faintly defined horizon was the North Star.

2

He had escaped. Above him, swaying slightly, were the black silhouettes of leaves; as his eyes became used to the dim light he saw a rough track leading downhill. He ran down the path intent on getting far away from the nest before morning brought the ant-hill to life. He ran until the first stirring of the morning breeze moved the grass blades at the side of the track and the cold light of dawn crept up from the horizon. He heard a distant churring and singing of cicadas in the rockery and was startled by the same song suddenly magnified a thousand times; he leapt away from the sound to the side of the track. Through the morning mist he saw the creature, as big as a bullock, which made the noise.

The cicada crouched, vigorously rasping out its deafening song. Curious to see how the creature made the noise, Dilke moved nearer to it. The cicada stopped in mid-song, appeared to sense the man's approach and suddenly, with a convulsive movement of its hind legs, it vanished into the lightening sky.

A clump of hollyhocks grew at the side of the track, soaring above Dilke like Eiffel towers. He decided that he had run far enough, climbed up the stalk of a plant, seated himself astride a jutting stem with his back against the trunk and waited for the sun. A ground mist lay across the lawn and the leaves below him were dotted with drops of dew like crystal igloos. He considered his situation.

16

This was a jungle peopled with creatures more savage than those known to man. If he was to survive he must find shelter, a place he could barricade: any hole or corner would not do.

The light of the rising sun slanted across the lawn, dispersing the mist. Its rays were caught in the domes of dew and split up into shimmering rainbows. Dilke could see all his garden, some of it still shadowed by the lime trees at the end of the lawn. He climbed farther up the hollyhock; the landscape lay drowsily under the June sun. He looked beyond his garden to the allotment. It lay on a slope and his eyes travelled over an area of rough fallow ground beyond which a planting of carrots had gone to seed, a green feathery plantation running up the slope and over the curve of the horizon like a tropical forest. And towering above the horizon was the angular shape of a garden shed. A tangle of honeysuckle crawled up its side and was heaped on top; a blue heat-haze softened its outlines and the sun glittered on the fallen blossoms which lay like snow in the corrugations of the sloping roof.

The exertions of climbing and a substance oozing from the pores of the plant made Dilke hot and sticky and he bathed in dew which had gathered in a watery blob at the junction of veins in a leaf. He pressed his hand through the surface tension of the drop into its interior and his body slid in after his hand and arm. He sat down inside it and rubbed his body briskly; it was cold but invigorating, like sitting inside a balloon filled with ice-water. After his bath he looked down from the edge of the leaf. Traffic was in full swing along the ants' trail that ran near the foot of the hollyhock; a spider dropped past the leaf on which Dilke stood in a fast controlled fall at the end of its thread; a drift of dandelion clocks floated slowly past, some of them twirling singly, some of them waltzing together in interlocked groups. One of the clocks hovered over Dilke, then slowly dropped in the still air above the leaf. The heavy seed-pod, suspended from a white head of delicate hollow filaments which gave it buoyancy, came swinging down. Dilke shoved the pod away. It hit the leaf and dragged along its surface, the hooks on the pod leaving raw green tracks behind them.

Again Dilke fixed his attention on the distant shed. In it there would be manmade things, amongst them he might find some sort of container in which he could live. Dilke made the decision: the shed looked about half a day's march away, if he started now he would be there before night. He took a long drink, descended the plant, waited till there was a break in the flow of ant traffic and ran across the track into the broken fallow ground.

He moved at a fast walking pace up the long slope to the wall of green foliage which marked the edge of the carrot plantation. The surface was very rough, with huge clods of earth and stones and a multitude of gullies that ran all ways. He travelled along the bottom of the gullies to conceal himself from foraging ants which he had seen marching on the horizon. At last he came out of this rough terrain; before him stretched smoother ground at the other side of which lay the plantation.

He set off across the plain leaving a low cloud of dust behind him.

The smoothness of the ground was broken by craters. When Dilke came to the first one he skirted its edge. Turning his head to see into the smooth-sided crater he saw a movement out of the corner of his eye: it was an ant following him at a sharp hunting trot. It too left a dust trail behind it; it too had come out of the rough ground from the north. It must have been tracking him for some time. Dilke ran round the curve of a crater, picked up a rock as big as his fist and threw it at the beast in the way one would seek to discourage a big dog. But this only provoked it: with a quick flourish of its antennae it jumped towards him over the edge of the crater, ran down the slope, then clambered up towards him. The crater was faced with small loose rocks and the ant lost its foot-hold. It slid back to the bottom of the hole. Suddenly, like a burst from a volcanic geyser, there was a flurry of sand in the crater bottom. The ant's movements became frantic: it fell and turned about, the sun flashing on its churning legs and armoured carapace. From the centre of the crater came two huge, hooked claws and part of the head of a submerged monster. The oiled, metallic pincers snapped shut on the desperate ant; head, claws, ant—all sank into the sand. There was a sound like that of sticks being broken, a last tiny flurry in the sand, and the sides of the crater became still and smooth. For a time Dilke stood transfixed. Then he ran towards the plantation, making wide detours around craters on the way.

He flung himself panting under the first plant. The dust which covered him from head to foot was streaked with sweat. His throat was parched, his forehead and shoulders were burnt by the sun but his mind kept returning to the sights and sounds which he had seen. Gradually his breath came more easily and after he had lain for some time looking up at the sky through the fronds of the carrots he resumed his march. He discovered that the carrots were planted in parallel lines. The lines ran north and south and he walked down one of the avenues. From the brow of the hill he saw the shed through the carrot tops, its wooden walls silvery grey with age, its green, panelled door taken from a demolished house. The allotment owner had died last year. His son-in-law was not a gardener and he had nailed two rough-sawn deal planks across the door to keep out children.

At last Dilke walked out of the plantation. The shed filled his whole field of vision; the surface of the huge door pitted with burst paint blisters, the new planks a raw yellow in the light of the evening sun.

He climbed the threshold, passed under the door and went inside. The light was dim, a gale rushed under the door and swept the floor clean of debris. Along the walls and in the corners of the shed were piled the collected tools and litter of a lifetime. Hoes, rakes, spades, a fishing-rod, a bicycle pump, stacks of plant-pots. In the fading light he could see shelves stacked with boxes and jam-jars. A bunch of rusting keys and hanks of raffia hung from nails. The light was dying fast and the roof overhead was like a black sky, with stars of light shining through nail holes in the corrugated sheets. He started down the long perspective of the plank floor looking for a home. In the corner, lying at an angle on a pile of sacks, was an old wooden box, its surface covered with inlaid

veneers, cracked and falling away. A glint of yellow near
the top caught his eye: recessed into the box was a brass
lock, the keyhole was covered by a heavy, sliding door.

Dilke had found a fortress.

3

He slept under a shard of broken plant-pot and woke to
see the sun striking across the front of the towering box.
It was transformed by the morning light into a building
of Byzantine splendour, the marquetry sparkling with yellow and rich reds and greens, the lock a glittering gold.
Its beauty stunned Dilke for a moment, then he scrambled
over the coarse sacking and started to climb. The box was
twelve inches high, the side up which he climbed lay back
at a slight angle and the cracks between the wood inlays
gave easy foot-holds. In places, whole sections of inlay
had fallen out, leaving ledges along which he could walk.
The thought of finding a safe place to live exhilarated him
and soon he reached the threshold of the lock and climbed
over its edge.

The thick cover over the keyhole was immovable: the
runners on which it rested were choked with rubble. He
dug at it with his hands, but quickly realized that without
some sort of tool he would be unable to free the door. He
sat down, his legs dangling over the edge of the platform
and looked for something suitable. The jam-jars on the
shelves above him were full of nails and seashells and the
seeds of plants. There was a packet of lump sugar next
to an enamelled mug and a mouth organ; the old man
must have spent a lot of time in here.

Dilke looked down to the floor. A tobacco tin full of panel pins had fallen from a shelf and burst open, scattering the nails over a wide area. They were like miniature crowbars: pointed at one end, with blunt heads at the other. He climbed down and picked out a pin which was as long as he was tall. He hefted it in his hand, pleased with its weight and rigidity; then as he turned to start the climb back to the lock he saw a pool of oil which had leaked from a can. He filled an empty seed-case with the oil, which had the consistency of cart-grease, and he returned with the bar and the grease to his lock. He cleared the door-runners, greased them, and, inserting the bar behind the thick brass door, he pulled on it till the veins stood out on his arms and neck.

Slowly the slab of metal moved, it moved more easily as it travelled on to the oiled surface and suddenly the aperture of the keyhole appeared; he strained at the lever until the slit was wide enough to admit his body. It was like the inside of an old mill, the huge beams and springs were covered with yellow dust. For years a key had been inserted and turned, particles of metal had been scraped off and they coated the lock mechanism and lay in drifts along the walls of the chamber. He ran his hand along a beam and examined the glittering metal on his palm.

He was exultant. He laughed aloud and, slapping his dusty hands together, he sprang out on to the platform. He cupped his hands around his mouth and whooped down the length of the shed.

This was a turning point. The world was still full of monstrous terrors, but looking down on the shed floor from his high shelf he thought for the first time that he might survive. His thoughts and efforts had been so much concentrated on entering the lock that he had not thought of food. Late afternoon found him with a place to sleep in safety but without supper to fill his belly. He made a quick excursion to the floor and foraged along the dust-filled cracks between the boards. Amongst the debris he found seeds which had spilled from jars and packets: turnip, tomato, radish, lettuce seeds; they ranged from the size of coconuts to the size of pumpkins and he split some open with a bar. Their flesh was fibrous and rather dry but his hunger was sharp and he was glad to carry some up to his shelf where he sat chewing and watching the night shift of insects appear. Cockroaches came out from the sacking at the foot of his tower and he heard the first peevish whine of a mosquito in the black roof.

Dilke kicked the chewed remnants of food over the edge of the platform and recalled his last briefing from the Head of Laboratories. 'After miniaturization, watch your diet, Captain Dilke. These drugs have been rigorously lab tested and I think we've got the side effects ironed out, but you may have trouble if your diet is unbalanced. Take adequate protein. Go easy on sugars.'

Dilke wondered how aphid's milk and turnip seeds would figure on his diet sheet. He felt a sudden desire for a smoke to round off the day and he promised himself that tomorrow he would look for tobacco; the old man must surely have been a smoker and there might be fragments of tobacco on some of the shelves. At dusk he entered the chamber and slid the door shut. He fell asleep with the muffled noise of insect traffic outside.

In the following days Dilke had no trouble finding food and drink: the seeds of plants were plentiful and water ran from a leaking barrel outside the hut. He shared the stream with his insect neighbours, approaching it warily, watching for predators.

A packet of carrot seeds had fallen to the floor. It leaned against the shed wall, the huge picture of carrots like a colossal sign-painting on the front of an Odeon. The packet had been opened, and then closed with a rusting paper-clip; it advertised last year's programme, 'Carter's Tested Seeds: Golden Glory Carrots'. Her Majesty had given her approval with a coat of arms twice the height of Dilke. Dampness and mildew had rotted the packet and Golden Glory had germinated. The pale shoots which pierced the paper were tender and as thick as Dilke's arm: he found them palatable. He also experimented with insect flesh: eggs and pupa and insects the size of hares. Inside the horny exteriors of these creatures he found a white flesh not unlike lobster meat. Sitting one afternoon on the sunlit platform, he cracked open the brittle casing of an insect's leg. The raw meat within was unappetizing but he chewed stolidly and gazed out into the shed. The

sun struck hot through the shed window and across the
floor. A vinegar bottle lay on its side and its lens-like
base concentrated the light into an incandescent spot
inside the bottle.

A barbecue!

He descended to the shed floor and killing an insect
with his bar he carried it up to the neck of the bottle. A
current of hot air met him when he got into the bottle
neck. He climbed down a tangle of spider's web which lay
in the neck and looped down into the interior. It was an
old web from last winter, the furnace-like heat had driven
the spider out and dehydrated its web so that it was no
longer sticky. Dilke approached the point of heat and
prodded the dead insect into its centre. Shielding his face
with his arm he watched it: the creature seemed to come
alive under the heat, its body and limbs jerked spasmod-
ically, and after a while a bubbling fluid oozed from its
joints. It smelt good and when he raked it out and broke
open its casing it tasted succulent. He burnt his fingers in
his impatience, and while waiting for the carcase to cool
he tried the experiment of setting fire to a length of web.
It smouldered and glowed, throwing off a quantity of
black smoke. He carried back to his fortress the remains
of the carcase and the burning rope, the smoke slowly
drifting up the side of the box with him as he climbed
from ledge to ledge. He broke off fragments of the wood
veneer with a crowbar, piled them in the corner of the
lock facia and set them alight. He sat till it was quite
dark enjoying the novelty of a warm fire and a hot dinner.
When moths, which were attracted to the spot of light,
endangered both Dilke and his fire by gusts from their
huge wings he moved it inside and closed the door, leaving a narrow gap to ventilate the chamber. He went to
sleep gazing up at the flames glinting on the brass ceiling.

Dilke's days now went in a routine way: replenish the
fire, using wood from the inlays and the husks of seeds;
go down to the water barrel to drink and to wash; carry
seeds back to the lock for breakfast; hunt down edible
insects and barbecue them.

One day he observed a cockroach laying her eggs. She

deposited them in flimsy containers which slowly hardened into stiff, brown cases. He followed her closely, ripped open a delicate sheath while it was still soft, then carried off eggs to the fire on the platform and cooked them in hot ashes.

The prodigality of nature in miniature set him thinking of the riches available to a race of his own size. To a man three hundred times smaller than his natural size, the earth would be three hundred times bigger; three hundred times richer.

As he ate he pictured a world of micro-people. Great harvests of insects eggs and plant seeds. New and as yet unknown sorts of food, the spores of moulds, the larger bacteria. Living inside fruit and vegetable like worms in the apple core, although that diet would be monotonous. A subterranean society, a take-over of the nests and the aphid herds of ants. The eviction of termites from their huge stalagmite buildings: ready-made skyscrapers, renovated, with cell walls removed to enlarge the chambers and with lifts installed. The hanging tree nests of wasps, a dividing wall down the middle, one half left for the insects to store their honey, the other for humans with access through the partition to the stored food.

Dilke finished his meal and leaned back against the sun-warmed door.

Living as parasites in the bodies of animals, elephants and the larger cattle. Thousands of humans living in an elephant, adjusting to its movements like sailors at sea. Whole societies living beneath the skin of a bull, anaesthetizing the area to prevent the irritation which would cause the animal to scratch and destroy the parasite cities. Surrounded by a storehouse of living protein, the flesh and the blood of their host. Feeding their sewage into the veins of the creature to filter through to the animal's main sewer.

Animals living placid and uneventful lives would make the best city states; they could be domesticated by giant humans, moronic, but literate enough to take instructions and living in superstitious fear of their little masters, terrified of their power to hurt and punish them, to poison their food and attack the sensitive tissues of their eyes and ears whilst they slept. They could protect as well as herd the docile elephants and cattle, hunting down carnivores which by killing a host animal would destroy a whole society of micro-humans; the eating of one bullock by one tiger could bring death to hundreds of people. The gross overgrown giants would be slave labourers on a gargantuan scale: quarrying and building and tilling the soil . . .

'Miniaturizing can save us from the major twentieth-century threat—overpopulation.'

Dilke remembered the long, intense face of Professor Mathis.

'This work we are doing is classified, Captain Dilke, though God knows why! You have been sent to me because you are in the secrets business and your experience fits you for the job—we want a trained communicator to give us a feedback of information. If you agree to help with this project your department has agreed to free you.' Mathis had removed his glasses and massaged an eye socket with a bony forefinger. 'I will be frank. We have perfected the technique on laboratory animals, but you would be the first man to be miniaturized. You would be the first man in a pioneer group, the first of a new society in which famine and territorial wars will be unknown . . .'

Dilke's memories were interrupted by the scrabbling of a wood louse which had been attracted to the base of the tower by the remnants of his meal. After snuffling in the coarse sacking, it started to climb the towering wall. Dilke kicked over one of the piles of stones which he had placed on the ledge, neat as water melons in a greengrocer's shop, to scare off climbing insects. They bounced down, peppering the foraging louse which lost its footing and dropped between the sacking mesh.

He had not kicked the stones down out of fear—he did not now think that every insect was dangerous—he had been curious to see what the louse would do, its panic amused him. He picked up a boulder in both hands and lobbed it out in a curve. It diminished in size till it vanished through the mesh, and he saw the sacking shake as the wood louse ran off under cover.

He stood up and stretched and looked out over the floor of the shed; his whole body was now tanned brown, hardened by exposure to heat and cold. He knew that the dangers which threatened him in this micro-world he could face rationally.

Dilke suddenly realized that the first part of his mission was completed. It was time to get in touch with Department 7A.

PART TWO

1

Dilke started his journey before sunrise. Shutting the door to the chamber and climbing down the front of the box, his hands and feet finding their way in the dark along the familiar ledges, he picked up a bar from amongst those which littered the floor and shouldered it. When he walked out from under the door the night wind had dropped, the moon and stars glittered in the lightening sky. Some thin clouds on the horizon glowed with pink light from the rising sun. It was going to be a hot day.

Dilke walked into one of the misty avenues of carrots and started his long march. He took his time, thinking of the message that he was going to send, pausing to watch the sun as it blazed over the horizon, fascinated by the inexorable opening of the awakening flowers. He changed the bar from shoulder to shoulder to ease its weight; though it was an encumbrance and had limited use as a weapon he felt comforted by its heavy, cold feel. By mid-morning he had reached his garden, leaving the plantation and plains and rough country of the allotment behind him. At noon he came to the rim of the rockery and he slid down its steep slopes and entered his house through a crack between the closed French windows.

This room in which he had lived, with its tufted carpet and Swedish furniture, now seemed impersonal and remote to him. He passed the wilting castor oil plant and walked through the forest of pillars which were the legs of the table and chairs from which he had once dined. He reached the edge of the carpet; the pile was head-high, its uneven surface covered with curling tendrils which tripped him. The way to his study lay diagonally across the carpet but he chose to take the long way on the teak surround.

On his study floor, beneath the desk, they had left a torch battery resting on a six-inch plastic tile. Dilke climbed up and found a miniature Morse transmitter cemented to the surface of the tile and wired to the battery. Despite its small size the instrument was, in Dilke's eyes, as big and crude as a dump truck. The rocker arm was chest-high and to operate it he had to lean on it with all his weight. At three forty-five by the wall clock he spelt out the slow, slow, quick, quick, slow of his code signature: 'Double O point two five', followed by the departmental cypher.

Slowly and laboriously: 00.25 CALLING DEPARTMENT 7A. PREPARE TO TAKE MESSAGE 0700 HOURS TOMORROW —he had lost count of days and dates. He repeated the message at half-hourly intervals till ten o'clock.

Throughout the day Dilke's thoughts had returned to the subject of weaponry: primitive weapons like spears would be inadequate against insects. Something more powerful like a skindiver's harpoon-gun? No, the velocity would be insufficient. But the crossbow principle was a good one, with the right design he might even make one from existing materials. Insects bodies were walking Meccano sets: tubes, thongs, joints, levers . . .

He remembered a display of medieval crossbows in the British Museum . . . if he could have one as a guide . . . He fell asleep beside the transmitter. He slept fitfully and dreamt that he was squinting along the sights of a huge, smoking machine-gun, vintage '14–18, hosing down a battalion of ants which streamed over the rim of the rockery.

His dream merged with reality: the rattle of the gun became a chattering message from the morse receiver: DEPT 7A TO 00.25 . . . DEPT 7A TO 00.25 . . . DEPT 7A TO 00.25 . . . ACKNOWLEDGE . . . DEPT . . . To stop the clatter Dilke replied 00.25 TO DEPT 7A. STAND BY TILL . . . he glanced at the wall clock, 0715 HRS. That gave him fifteen minutes to compose his message.

At seven fifteen he began his report. 00.25 REPORTING

TO DEPT 7A. MISSION SUCCESSFUL. SURVIVAL PROVED
POSSIBLE. COMMENCE SECOND STAGE. DELIVER EQUIP-
MENT AND PERSONNEL AS FOLLOWS——ONE ENTOMOLO-
GIST. ONE PORTABLE TWO-WAY RADIO. TWO MACHETES.
PHOTOGRAPHS OF ALL BRIT MUS CROSSBOWS BOTH DIS-
MANTLED AND ASSEMBLED. CROSSBOW PHOTOGRAPHS TO
BE ONE THREE HUNDREDTH SIZE. DELIVER TO THIS AD-
DRESS. WINDOW SEAT. WILL CONTACT YOU FOR DELIVERY
DATE THREE DAY'S TIME, END OF MESSAGE. GIVE SLOW
REPEAT.

It took him thirty minutes to spell it out and his chest
and arms ached with the strain. The repeat came back in
sixty seconds.

Dilke spent the next three days pottering about his
house. He discovered a good route from the floor to the
window seat: an inclined footway along the wire to the
indoor TV aerial. He looked for hours at his garden
through the huge picture window. The view was the
same one he had so often seen before he was miniaturized;
he could almost forget that he was now only 0.25″ tall.
But there were signs in the house and the garden of the
change that had taken place: the lawn had not been cut
for a month, dust lay thick on the wide window seat, the
glass was streaked and spotted with dirt and a spider had
set up house in a corner of the window-frame. He could
never look at the garden in the same way again: his eyes
now searched for alternative ways up the face of the
rockery, the hollyhocks he knew to be bigger than red-
woods, and he dared not walk along the western edge of
the lawn for fear of soldier ants.

Promptly on time on the third morning the receiver
rattled out its message from Intelligence.

It gave the date of message transmission. It promised
to expedite his order. It gave the date of delivery. It
signed off.

Dilke would have his new man and his equipment in
three weeks. He decided to return to the place he now
thought of as home: the lock chamber in the box in the
allotment hut. For three weeks he slept, drank, ate and
explored the hut, climbing its walls and wandering along
its shelves. He found a box full of fishing gear: huge coils
of line, gigantic hooks, lead weights as big as barges. On

too big a scale to be useful to Dilke, but he searched for and found some nylon line of one-pound breaking strain, some size twenty fresh-water hooks and some split-shot leads twice as big as his head. The line was rather too heavy for a climbing-rope but he hitched one end to a nail head and dropped the coil over the shelf edge, it hit the ground with a thud and spilled out in loops and curls across the floor. He manhandled two hooks and half a dozen shots to the edge of the shelf and sent them crashing after the rope; then he climbed down. He left the hooks and lead weights lying but he burned through the rope and made it up into coils. One he tied to a bar inside the chamber letting it hang down to the floor of the shed: an alternative way to climb the face of the box, and a way to haul things up to the platform. The other coils he stored neatly in the chamber.

As the arrival time of the new micro-man came nearer Dilke became restless. On the evening before his journey to meet him he looked at the bare quarters, trying to see them through the eyes of a newcomer; then he tidied up the platform and chamber and threw out the rubbish which had accumulated. He took an evening walk to the shed door and looked northwards towards the house beyond the ridge. The sun set behind the plantation; he wished it was morning so that he could start the journey.

2

Dilke set out before dawn, bar on shoulder, a coil of rope round his chest. This time he travelled without pausing to watch the sun rise or the flowers open. He entered through the French windows, travelled under the dying castor oil plant and hurried up the inclined TV wire.

This was to be his first meeting with a man for almost two months. He had faced the hazards of this enormous frontier world stoically and the need to survive had fixed his attention on day-to-day problems. It had been a solitary life and he had felt no need for a companion. But now he was excited at the prospect of meeting one and eager to see what sort of man he would be.

The sun struck Dilke in the eyes when his head came above the level of the window seat. Then he saw the man stretched out, his hands behind his head, lying on a bundle of coarse blankets. He was surrounded by a clutter of gear, like a student begging a lift to the South of France. He lay with crossed legs and stared up at a spider which crouched in its funnel web above his head. Dilke watched the spider apprehensively until it slowly backed into the shadow of the web's entrance. He caught his breath with relief, then felt a stir of exasperation at the man's casual posture.

Dilke walked forward.

The man sat up slowly and clambered to his feet. He was tall, lanky, and bony shouldered. Under a flop of dark hair his eyes were young and friendly, his long face wore a smile. He extended his right hand, 'Mr Dilke, I presume.'

Dilke's face was stiff.

What the hell had they done now? He had asked for a man and they'd sent him a fatuous boy. What good was this fine sprig to him? He must be barely twenty-one; wet out of university.

Dilke's expectations died a death. He seethed at this latest idiocy of head office.

'My name is Henry Scott-Milne.'

It bloody would be!

Dilke shook the hand perfunctorily and then picked up some of the gear and moved it away from the vicinity of the web. Scott-Milne brought along the rest of the equipment, put it down, and stood and looked expectantly at Dilke. He was perplexed by Dilke's manner but he retained his expression of easy goodwill. Dilke looked blankly at the equipment, fighting down his anger, but

finally said, 'Well, let's check over the stuff.' Scott-Milne
bent quickly to the bundle of blankets, pulled at a slip-
knot, jerked the end of a blanket and out rolled two
heavy machetes; Dilke's expression brightened. He picked
up one of them, it was all steel, from handle to tip;
rather blunt, but that could soon be mended. He held it
high and dropped it, point first; it clunked into the wood
and remained standing erect.

"The radio?'

Scott-Milne unwrapped a plastic bag. The radio was
primitive and not very portable but it would be a sight
better than the Morse tapper. While Dilke was turning
over the radio in his hands, Scott-Milne untied a large
portfolio. He opened it out flat revealing the first of a
pile of photographs of crossbows. He dug to the bottom
of the pile, extracted a sheet and offered it to Dilke. 'Oh,'
he smiled, 'I should have shown you this before. My cre-
dentials.'

The sheet was a microfilmed letter from head office, the
characters as big as eggs. There was a short introduction
in officialese from Major Price, Head of Department 7A,
followed by a potted biography of Scott-Milne.

While Dilke read them, the subject of the notes quietly
laid out the crossbow photographs in a row.

Name: Henry Scott-Milne.
Code Number: 00.25/2.
Age: 25 years.
Birthplace: Bath, England.
Education: Summerhill. Cambridge.
Honours Degrees: Zoology. Mathematics.
Rowing Blue.
Family Background: Father—Professor William
Scott-Milne—Biologist.
Grandfather—Joseph Scott-Milne—associate of T.
H. Huxley.
The family has a distinguished scholastic history
with special interest in science and biology.
General Notes: Published first book, *Social Insects
and their Ecological Niche,* when seventeen. Has
lectured extensively.

Zoologist at Cambridge.
Antarctic Expeditions: 1965, 1968.

Dilke looked up from the letter.

The crossbows were printed on thick sheets of transparent acetate and Scott-Milne had propped them against
the window so that the images could be seen against the
light and he crouched with his back to Dilke examining
one of them.

The last of Dilke's anger ebbed away leaving a residue
of embarrassment.

He was searching for words to make amends for his
churlish manner when the young man turned and said,
'Fascinating pictures; but what are they for?'

'That's something we can talk about later,' said Dilke,
'but first of all, Henry, if you find me a bit unsociable,
then please put it down to the fact that I've been living
alone—one gets a bit hermit-like.'

Scott-Milne made deprecating noises.

'My name is Mathew, call me Mat if you like. Let me
tell you what I've been doing here . . .'

If they had started immediately they might have made the
journey back to the shack before night but Dilke put off
the journey till next day, giving himself time to find out
more about Henry Scott-Milne and prepare him for his
new life.

His companion was eager to see this microscopic world
from the inside; his knowledge was clearly encyclopaedic,
like that of an older man, yet his enthusiasm and his
humour were those of an undergraduate. Dilke needed
someone whose knowledge of micro-life would enable
him to work out a survival code based on pre-knowledge
rather than hit-and-miss experience; but he also needed a
man who could fend for himself.

Scott-Milne's Antarctic trips interested Dilke and he
questioned him about his part in them. As zoologist Scott-
Milne had found himself in charge of the dogs and he had
fed them on seal-meat. So his duties as zoologist and
entomologist had widened to include those of dog-keeper
and butcher—and part-time cook. As they talked on

into the evening Dilke's spirits rose with each new indication of Henry Scott-Milne's resourcefulness.

Dilke described some of his own experiences. Pointing
through the window at the now darkening landscape he
traced for Scott-Milne the route through his garden and
into the allotment. When it was quite dark they lay rolled
in the coarse blankets.

Dilke's conversational barrier was now down; seven
weeks of solitude had built up a head of talk which he
now dissipated by describing all that had happened to him
since his miniaturization.

They lay cocooned in blankets, looking through the
window at the night sky. Mathew Dilke luxuriated in the
sensations of blanket warmth and companionship.

He described his pursuit and capture by ants and his
escape from their nest. Scott-Milne's excitement grew as
he listened; ant life was his special subject and he re-
peatedly interrupted Dilke's narrative to question him.
Clearly, if Dilke had offered to take him to the ant
colony Henry Scott-Milne would have been happy to go
immediately.

His knowledge of and respect for ants became clear as
he described them: the age of the species, their diversity,
the complexity of their societies, the subtleties of their
intellect. He described their farming methods; the aphid
dairy farms; the cultivation of soil near the nests and the
growing of seed-bearing plants on this ground; the storing
of leaves in the nests on which moulds grew which then
became food for the colony.

Dilke was disarmed by Scott-Milne's lack of affecta-
tion: he used a language which was almost self-con-
sciously free of jargon and technical terms. The words
'bugs' and 'ladybirds' and 'hoppers' occurred frequently.

'Did you know, Mathew, that ants have been going for
thirty-five million years? That's nearly thirty-five times as
long as man has been on earth. Ants are perhaps the most
ubiquitous creatures alive: they range over the whole
world between extreme Arctic and Antarctic.' At last they
slept.

Dilke awoke and rolled out of his blanket. Henry lay, his
head tucked down, only his mop of hair showing. Dilke

knew that the drugs could have a depressant effect so he left him to sleep. He quietly packed their gear, roping up the portfolio and rolling the radio in his blanket. Henry was wakened by the rasping sound of one machete blade being sharpened against the other. He lay for a minute and watched Dilke. The big brown man had jammed the point of one of the heavy knives in a crack in the wood and gripped the handle between his knees. He was bent double over the knife, grinding the other machete along it with the long, purposeful sweeps that Henry had seen used by primitive men like Eskimos and aborigines.

The younger man was suddenly conscious of the pallor of his own skin; he felt a touch of apprehension about the future, and he felt drained of conversation after last night's talking marathon.

The rhythmic sound of sharpening had an hypnotic effect and he felt his eyelids drooping. He shook his head and worked with his knuckles to clear his eyes of sleep.

'Hello,' he called.

Dilke turned and grinned. 'It's a great day.' He spoke with a stage Irish accent. 'Would you care for a walk in the garden?'

They shared out the kit. Dilke devised a rope harness for the portfolio and carried it on his back. The wind that blew over the edge of the rockery caught the portfolio and gave him some trouble but he walked at an angle till they came to the shelter of the daisy forest. The forest had changed since he first ran through it. The grass blades and daisies now towered high overhead, the grass cuttings which had littered the ground had decayed or been carried away by insects. It was free of debris underfoot and they walked in file between the daisy stalks, Dilke leading, and chopping at them as he went with his new knife. The machete swung in arcs, the dappled sunlight flashing off its honed edge. The blade bit into the stalks with a thud and Dilke freed it with a jerk of the wrist, celebrating his pleasure in his new weapon by leaving a trail of wounded daisies.

They made a detour across the ant lion plain to avoid a party of hunting ants and entered the carrot patch. They toiled up the slope, the ropes holding the heavy portfolio cut into Dilke's shoulders. Henry followed one pace behind, carrying the radio; it was heavy and the long walk had tired him, an ache started in the small of his back.

Both men sweated profusely. A breeze caught them as they came over a rise in the ground, blowing gently through the green carrot tops, and Dilke stopped for a moment to enjoy it. Leaning forward against the weight of his burden he looked down the curving rows of plants, like an avenue of trees bordering a country road. Round the curve of the road he saw a flash of red between the foliage; they stepped forward again and were enveloped by the heat lying in the valleys. As they reached the bottom of the slope Dilke raised his eyes from the rough track and saw something which stopped him in midstride. A London double-decker bus. It was standing with its front stuck out into the avenue as if about to turn in from a side-road.

The sweat ran into Dilke's eyes and he blinked and rubbed it away impatiently with his forearm. He heard an exclamation behind him and a thud as Henry dropped his pack.

ROUTE 73: Park Lane/Marble/Arch/Oxford Circus. SSSCHWEPPESSSS was crudely screen-printed along its side.

Both men stood staring at the red bus, then Dilke took slow steps towards it.

Henry was completely disoriented, his eyes wide, like a man in the grip of hallucinations.

Through the windows of the lower deck they saw a sudden movement.

The illusion was complete: a No. 73 bus—with passengers—turning into a main road. But the engine made no sound and there was something wrong with the scale of the bus and something odd about its proportions.

Dilke approached it as though it might explode in his face; then he dropped the pack from his back, laid back his head and gave a shout of laughter.

Henry watched with astonishment; Dilke staggered to the bus side and hit it with the handle of his machete. Each blow made a dull thud and a dozen infant spiders scuttled out of the rear entrance and ran like monkeys up the nearest carrot.

The bus was solid lead.

Henry followed Dilke into its interior, it was a hollow shell with walls battleship thick; collapsed bubbles of soft metal pitted its smooth surface. On the outside, a thick ridge of metal ran down the centre of the bus casting where the two halves of the mould had met.

Now all was clear, and they could fit this crude facsimile into their scheme of things; they lay down to rest. For the first time Henry Scott-Milne truly knew how small he was: smaller—much smaller—than a child's toy. He turned his head and looked at Mathew Dilke who lay with closed eyes, chewing at a fibre of grass; unperturbed. Scott-Milne felt reassured.

When they reached the hut it was sunset. Dilke was tired and Scott-Milne exhausted. They left the heavier things at the bottom of the box, Dilke climbed ahead with the blankets and his machete and the younger man climbed behind him. The fire was out, the chamber was cold, they wrapped their blankets about them and fell asleep.

Next day Dilke was gratified by Henry's enthusiasm for his quarters ('Not so much a penthouse more a bed-sit') and for the routine that he had devised. He took Henry on a tour: down the face of the box to bathe and drink at the stream, out to the hut threshold to look across the forest of carrots through which they had travelled the previous day. And at midday when the sun was at its height he initiated him into the wonder of his solar barbecue.

After dining off grilled leg of earwig they climbed the box front and relit the fire on the platform, and while Dilke fiddled with the radio Henry searched the floor near the base of the tower for fuel; fragments of wood, dried seeds and brittle cast-off insect cases. He hauled them up to the platform with the rope and stacked them near the fire.

The radio transmitter was silent, Dilke undid the primitive catches which held the back in place and poked around inside until he was rewarded by a burst of static. Though its system was rudimentary and its finish was crude the radio now functioned and next morning Dilke spoke to the controller of Department 7A.

Major Maurice Price sounded just as he had before

Dilke had been miniaturized. As they talked Dilke saw in
his imagination the major's face: malaria-yellow skin,
thick black eyebrows, clipped scrubby moustache covering
the whole of his long top lip. A filing-cabinet warrior who
held a season ticket to every Business Efficiency Exhibi-
tion, had two girls keeping a wall-to-wall Critical Path
Analysis Chart up to date, and was called 'Prim Price' behind his back because of a spinsterish concern for pro-
cedural trivialities. He kept a rack of pipes on his desk
to show that he was a thinking man: Dilke had never
liked him.

Dilke dictated a cable to Mr. William Olsen, Assistant
Senior Game Warden, Kenya Game Reserve, Kenya. It
was an invitation to see big game of a sort Olsen had
never seen before, it asked for his help and invited him
to contact Major Price for further information. And, to
Price, Dilke vouched for Olsen's background and charac-
ter and asked him to do all he could to persuade Olsen
to join Scott-Milne and himself.

Both men then got down to making a crossbow. They
chose from the crossbow pictures the bow with the simplest
construction and set out to copy it in the materials which
they had to hand. The spine and stock of the bow were
made from a fine-grained piece of wooden inlay from the
box front; Dilke roughly shaped it with a machete and
then smoothed it with the file-like edge of an insect's leg.
They utilized a curved section from the inside of a wood
louse for the arch of the bow, and the bowstring was
made from a piece of monofilament fishing-line about one
and a half millimetres long.

The getting of the bow's arch demonstrated Henry's
entomological knowledge and his skill as a butcher.

Amongst the discarded leftovers beneath a spider's web
they found several insect parts which were suitable in size
and shape for the bow; but when bent to test their resilience they snapped under pressure, the material had lost
its moisture content and had become brittle. Henry iden-
tified them as parts of a wood louse and they searched for
one of the right size to give them a piece which was not
dehydrated. They followed a solitary louse trundling down
the shed floor till it led to a herd cropping off a mildewed
newspaper in a dark corner of the shed. The lice were

packed close together, their blue-black backs touching, their pale legs moving slowly as they pastured on the *News of the World*. Henry picked out one about four millimetres long and strode through the herd towards it. The lice scattered in alarm and Henry ran beside the one he had chosen, gripped it under the edge of its curved armour-plating and neatly jerked it on to its back. The creature promptly curled into a ball and Henry forced the blade of his machete between the plates of its belly. The legs of the upturned louse raced frantically, it fell open as if a hinge had been broken and after Henry had slaughtered it he cut from its carcase the part which they needed for the crossbow. Dilke was impressed by his adroitness and found that the fresh-killed beast had provided a bow spring which was the right size and had the necessary resilience.

Having finished their bow they set off with some excitement next morning to try it out. Concealing themselves near the stream which ran from the water butt they waited for a suitable victim.

Sounds of running water and the early morning flight of wasps filled the air. A mob of grasshoppers came down to drink, the slanting light of the early sun gleaming on their angular bodies. Dilke aimed his first shot at the middle of the nearest hopper. The bolt went with good velocity but hit the creature low in the body, it glanced off the smooth plating and plunged into the shallow stream throwing up a spray of water. The insect was startled by the blow and it sprang into the air and vanished. Dilke's second shot was better, but though it hit a hopper squarely on the thorax it failed to penetrate. The creature was knocked sideways and almost fell, then it left its companions by the stream and stood sulkily alone. The wooden bolts were too light and Henry suggested that panel pins cut to length might be more effective.

A caterpillar humped its way along a leaf above the stream. Dilke shot a bolt at the soft-skinned creature which passed clean through its body; its movements stopped and it rolled slowly down the curved surface of the leaf, its brilliant green back and pale-green belly flashing as it rolled. It fell into the shadows in a shower of water. Then, to their astonishment, it righted itself and started its undulating journey again—a little more slowly, but otherwise unchanged. They were not the only observers of the caterpillar: a hunting wasp which had come to drink on the other side of the stream suddenly took a dozen running steps, flew off low over the water and with a noise like a buzz-saw mounted the caterpillar. Its legs clutched the bolster-like shape, the tip of its abdomen was raised high then brought flashing down, plunging its sting into the soft body. It withdrew the sting, spurting amber venom, and plunged it in twice more, the caterpillar rolled convulsively each time then lay still. The wasp retained its hold and with a blur of wings which rippled the surface of the stream it rose with its victim and lurched slowly and laboriously into the air.

Henry was the first to speak. 'By God! that's it, Mathew. That's the answer. Even if we penetrate these creatures many of them will be unharmed by a simple bolt. We must do it like that . . .' and he pointed to where the wasp disappeared among the honeysuckle leaves. They reconsidered the whole problem. Clearly they couldn't use wasp stings but they could make their own; and instead of wasp venom they could use poison from the jungle of nettles which grew against the hut side.

They returned to the spare-parts depot in the old spider's web and raked out dozens of tubes, the remains of insects' legs, which they carried to the edge of the stream. They stuck the ends into soft yellow clay and laid them in the sun to let the plugs harden, sealing one end. Then they climbed on to a nettle leaf and filled the tubes; Dilke struck the tips of the stings with the back of his heavy machete and the brittle glass-like spears snapped at the base. Henry carefully decanted the liquid into the hollow tubes and plugged the ends with clay. They sat on the leaf and waited for their first victim to come to the water.

A dung beetle abandoned its huge load to drink. The poisoned bolt was wonderfully effective. The weight of the liquid poison gave it extra penetrating power and the insect was killed or paralysed almost instantly. It was a convincing test case, for the beetle was heavily armoured. They took turns to shoot at a mixed mob of hoppers and

aphids. Their shooting was erratic because not all the
tubes were straight and some of the bolts swerved in
flight.

Ironically, one of their victims was a hunting wasp; it
came to the same watering-place as the wasp which had
inspired Henry. It took a little time to die, its erratic buzzing and spinning as it floated downstream frightening away
the more timid insects.

During their discussions about crossbow-making Dilke
discovered that his ideas about size and distance had become very muddled. When in his garden he alternated between thinking of the measurements he had known when
his garden was thirty feet long and the distance which he
now travelled, in which his garden seemed to be several
miles long.

Though Henry had occasionally found it difficult to
adapt emotionally to the new scale, in the abstract he
took to it immediately: a life spent thinking in fractions
of a millimetre had prepared him for a micro-world.

'What we want is a range of at least a hundred yards
if this crossbow is going to be any good,' said Dilke.

'Yards, Mathew?' laughed Henry. 'What we want is a
standard system of measurement if we're going to have a
meaningful way of talking about distance. What I mean is
that if we're going to relate the world of head office and
our world then we'll have to use a set of measurements
which will be common to both worlds yet which are fine
enough to be of use to you and me. I think it's typical of
British insularity that we're coded as 00.25 of an *inch:*
I'll bet your Major Price was behind that.'

They were talking on the ledge of the bed-sit; the
evening air was cool and they had a good leaping fire
going.

'Let us go metric. Look, Mathew,' lectured Henry, 'we
are about one three-hundred of our original size—that is
to say: You were 6 feet, you are now 00.25 of an inch,
which is a quarter of an inch. A quarter of an inch goes
into 6 feet 288 times. That's near enough 300: in other
words, one foot of our old world is now 300 feet. Your
garden, which I would guess was 30 feet long, is now like
9,000 feet long to us.' Henry paused to do mental arith-

metic. 'Let's say a mile is roughly 5,000 feet, then that makes your garden almost 2 miles long. And let's say the allotment is 75 feet long, about five miles to us, that makes it roughly 7 miles from here to your house, *to us*.

'But this is the interesting thing: you were 6 *feet* tall, you are now 6 *millimetres* tall. If we think in terms of millimetres instead of feet we have an easy way to talk about distances. For instance . . . ' Henry pointed over the edge of the platform at the shed floor which lay in darkness, 'the floor is about 150 millimetres below us—that would have been 150 feet by our old standards.'

Henry now talked quickly, as if at a lectern, impatiently flicking back his dark hair when it fell into his eyes.

'We could go on to centimetres and decimetres but it might be better to keep it simple and stick to millimetres. We can use decimals to express fractions of a millimetre: you are 6 millimetres, I am about 5.95 millimetres . . . ' Henry paused for breath. 'Our walking speed is about 15,000 millimetres an hour; our running speed is about 50,000 millimetres an hour. A normal-sized man walking at 3 miles per hour would seem to us to be travelling at about 1,000 miles per hour . . .' He pulled a stick out of the fire, knocked out the flames on the platform edge and drew figures on the smooth yellow surface of the door.

OBJECT	Actual speed (miles)	Apparent speed to us
Normal man	3 m.p.h.	1,000 m.p.h.
Vehicle	30 m.p.h.	10,000 m.p.h.
Jet plane	1,000 m.p.h.	300,000 m.p.h

Henry gazed abstractedly at the box. He wrote beneath it in big letters: ONE MILLIMETRE=ONE FOOT, then turned to Dilke with a wide smile. 'I've run out of steam.'

He speared the charcoal stick out into the blackness and came and squatted by the fire, 'As you say, Mathew, what we want is a crossbow with a range of at least 300 millimetres.'

On the following evening Dilke revealed his thoughts on the sort of life future micro-men might have.

'There's no food shortage, that's certain.' Dilke gazed into a steaming bowl made from a beetle's shell and poked at the half submerged seeds, sliced bean shoots and insect eggs. He recalled some of Professor Mathis's views on micro-populations and his belief that mass miniaturization could solve the problem of overpopulation.

'I think Mathis is too sanguine,' Henry drily interposed. 'If they don't lower the birth-rate the increase will soon negate the advantage of a bigger food supply. But they may be buying time—if they can reduce the pressure till the end of the century it gives them the chance to come up with something else.'

'You don't sound at all optimistic, Henry.'

'Just realistic, Mathew.' Henry fed sticks into the fire and sat back. 'These population trends are common to all forms of life: the graph goes up when conditions are right and comes down when they're not—though I think man has more in common with the suicidal lemming, than with other beasts.

'The big jump in the population of man started around 25000 B.C. with the invention of the clay pot and of missiles—which is just about where *we've* got to . . .' he nodded at the bowl and the crossbow. 'Before that there was enormous mortality through drinking blood and eating putrid flesh and burnt meat—stewing food sterilized it. And weapons reduced deaths from hunting dangerous animals. Ever since then, the increase has accelerated, till now it's up to fifty millions a year.'

'Well, we've got to try *something,* then.' Dilke looked up sharply through the steam.

'Of course. But don't worry Mathew, if this doesn't work there is always war, famine, pestilence, disease . . . acts of God and man. And I'm not really a pessimist. It's a slow, slow business; even if we bomb each other into the stone age we can't destroy all recorded knowledge, and the next log will get a flying start when they dig it all up.'

Dilke silently paddled the stew round the pot then said

with mild exasperation, 'Why the hell did you come on this jaunt, then?'

'I was asked,' Henry replied. 'And I wanted to be the first entomologist to meet *Aculeata formicidae* face to face.'

Dilke frowned.

'The ant, Mathew,' Henry explained.

3

Head office rang through next day.

Olsen was to join them. He was under sedation and would be ready to be picked up in ten days.

Henry put ten charcoal strokes on the door and as each day passed he crossed one out. On the evening before the rendezvous Dilke talked a good deal about Olsen.

Bill Olsen: an Anglo-Dane, son of a bankrupt tobacco farmer. They first met in a bar in Lagos when Dilke was keeping watch on a Chinese Peoples Republic Agricultural Delegation—and Olsen was resting between Rich American Trophy Hunters. When the C.P.R.A.D. left, the two men went up-country and safaried around for a while. For several years afterwards Dilke spent his vacations with Olsen. They both liked heat, rough country, hunting and boozing. When hunting went out of favour in East Africa Olsen took a job with the Kenya Game Preservation Reserve as a senior warden—'poacher turned gamekeeper', some said. Hippo and elephant overcrowded the reserve and Olsen was mostly employed in culling. In a letter to Dilke he had complained that his boss was a German conservation nut. Olsen found red tape irksome.

Henry began to wonder if he was going to get along with Olsen.

Dilke sat by the fire wrapping the handle of his machete with fishing-line. He had unravelled a length of multi-strand line and was carefully wrapping a strand round the metal handle. He talked of the villages up in the Gorilla highlands; of the sort of life the villagers lived and of their friendliness; of the drinking and the drumming and the dancing. He carefully wound the line in neat rows as he talked, grunting occasionally when he pulled it tight, remembering the trips through the sunburnt country, the black people, the thatched huts sitting like beehives on the hillsides . . . He heard a drumming so clearly that it could have been real, an ululating cry so real that it could have come from a village in a valley.

He looked up from the knife, Henry sat opposite, staring at him, his head turned a little to one side, listening . . .

Dilke dropped the knife, scrambled to his feet, cupped his hands round his mouth and shouted 'Bill!' He pulled the short word out; holding the sound for several seconds then he jumped to the platform edge and looked down to the shed floor, shielding his eyes from the glare of the fire. On the floor far below a figure squatted by a hollow seed-case shaped like a calabash. The beat of the drum grew quicker and louder till the hands of the man moved in a blur of speed. Then they stopped. There was a pause of seconds and a deep, measured voice spoke into the silence, intoning the words as if speaking a litany.

'Nakusalimu ndugu yangu. Nimekuja kwako kwa salama na amani.'

Dilke recognized the Swahili greeting of a stranger come to visit.

The greeting was followed by a shout of hoarse laughter, Dilke vaulted over the lip of the platform before the laughter stopped echoing from the shed walls, he took the rope in his hands and descended rapidly to the floor, like a rock climber going down a cliff face.

The light was now almost gone, but Henry saw Dilke hit the floor and run towards the drummer. The men paused for a moment before shaking hands and hammering each other on the back; then they turned and walked towards the tower. Henry heard the sounds of garbled talk and bursts of laughter, which grew clearer as the men climbed higher up the box face. A brown hand took hold of the platform edge, a second hand appeared and placed a polythene demijohn on the platform.

Olsen hauled himself up and stood erect. He was suddenly silent and he gazed at Henry steadily and without expression. Both men remained silent until Dilke clambered up and said, 'Henry this is Bill Olsen, Bill this is Henry Scott-Milne,' then Olsen stepped forward and shook hands. He was a much shorter man than Dilke, but as broad; his medium height and wide shoulders gave him a square appearance and' he stood on slightly bowed legs. He had a beat-up Jean Gabin face rather too big for his body; his hair was blond, streaked with bleached white strands.

The extraordinary thing about him was his colouring. His face had been burnt brick-red by the African sun but the rest of him was a patchwork of brown and white like a Hereford bull. His bush shirt and shorts had kept his pale skin from the sun and his feet were laced with a white filigree from the straps of his sandals. A puckered scar started in the brown of his neck and ran across his chest as if he had been run through a sewing machine.

'How the hell did you get here?' cried Dilke.

'*Walked,* you soft sod. Straight down Park Lane, and I brought my luggage with me!' Bill Olsen reached out a hand and picked up the polythene container.

'Yes, but how did you find us?' insisted Dilke.

'Followed you; a one-eyed Kaffir with his head in a sack could have seen your tracks. Here—have a go at this, old man,' he uncapped the big polythene bottle and handed it to Dilke. The swirling liquid hiccuped twice and Dilke put his nose to the neck of the bottle then grinned and raised it to his mouth. Henry watched his Adam's apple rise and fall in jerks, then Dilke wiped his mouth with the back of his hand, wiped the neck with his palm and handed it across to him.

Henry put the bottle to his lips and sipped at its contents. The neat whisky caught at his throat and he burst into a paroxysm of coughing; tears ran from his eyes.

Bill Olsen rescued the bottle and looked at him in a friendly way, 'You should take more water with it, my old lad.'

'But why are you a day early? You weren't due until tomorrow.'

'It's Saturday today and I said they could drop me off on Friday night and save the week-end of the guy who was doing the delivery job. Christ! You were right about the game, Mat. The place is alive with it: millions of ants and herds of those green things. How are you fixed for guns? You'll need a .470 Bloch and Steiner to stop some of the brutes, they've got plates on them like bloody tanks.'

Henry brought out the crossbow and gave it to Olsen who examined it with interest but clearly thought it was inadequate until they explained the use of the poisoned bolts. He caressed its stock with his hand, worked the cocking lever, and put it to his shoulder. 'It's very good,' he said, 'it might be better to hinge the lever a bit farther back and you should try to cut out that squeak. Is this the only one you have?'

'The only one,' said Dilke.

'I'll start on number two tomorrow,' said Olsen.

They moved indoors away from the moths and took the fire with them. The two older men settled down to a session of reminiscence and bottle passing. Henry sat quietly and watched them, contributing laughter to Bill Olsen's more outrageous stories and keeping the fire going. As the hours passed a sadness came over him; these men talked of friends and places and past experiences as if they still lived in the world they had known. He fell asleep with Bill Olsen's voice in his ears; English, with Danish and American overtones, spiced with obscenities.

Henry woke early and saw only Dilke asleep in the chamber, through the door he saw Olsen's square shape standing on the platform edge; as he watched, Olsen slowly brought the bow to his shoulder and fired.

'Any luck?' Henry asked.

Bill Olsen swung round 'No, no luck at all, Henry, these bolts are the big problem.' He was quieter than he had been on the previous night, though he seemed to suffer no ill effects from the drinking.

He asked Henry to help him get parts for a new bow and they talked together until they heard a long yawn from the lock interior. Bill Olsen raised his voice and called, 'Get up you lazy bastard!' and Dilke came out, his eyes screwed up against the grey morning light. He sat down heavily by the fire and in reply to Olsen's 'How are you feeling?' answered, 'Out of practice.'

They went to the stream and Dilke revived after a cold swim. As they re-entered the shed they saw the box in the distance. The morning sun revealed its full Byzantine glory, just as Dilke had first seen it. All three men stopped to stare. Then Olsen stepped forward. 'Come on men, let's get back to the Kremlin, I'm hungry.'

After breakfast Bill and Henry went off to find crossbow parts: to the web for bolts and a lever and to the mouldering slopes of the *News of the World* for a bow. Henry dispatched a wood louse and cut out the bow spring; Bill Olsen's face showed surprise at finding this butcher's skill in one he had thought so young. Henry killed and dissected two more lice and handed the three bow springs over: 'There's a choice of size for you, Bill.' They worked together on the new bow; in general it was much like the first one but with two important differences: the bow spring was much bigger, almost two millimetres wide; and Olsen fitted a sighting tube. There were also refinements in the shape of its stock and in its dimensions which made it much nicer to handle and which improved its performance.

Dilke was trying to mend the radio which had gone dead once more. As he did so he watched the two men. They were engrossed in their project and he was glad to see that the coldness which he had sensed between them had gone and that now they worked well together in spite of their different personalities. Henry had provided the adhesive, which Olsen needed to attach the sighting tube to the crossbow, by killing a small spider and using the fluid from its spinning gland. Henry stood with his foot on the creature's abdomen, like a man with a bright, red football, pressing out a milky fluid, while Bill Olsen ran the sighting tube along its spinnerettes, smearing the tube with adhesive. They attached it, and all three descended to the shed floor to test its accuracy and to do a little competitive target practice.

Crossbow Mark II exceeded the range of Dilke's first

bow by a clear two hundred millimetres, achieving a flight of almost five hundred millimetres. They found that the sighting tube was inaccurate so they removed it and returned to the more primitive method which Dilke had devised. In addition to his crossbow making, Bill Olsen's professionalism showed itself in other ways: he organized their living conditions like a man setting up camp in the bush. He rationalized the Kremlin cooking arrangements —the name had stuck—he rigged up a cooking spit over the platform fire and he hauled up containers to the platform and stored water in them. He sent Henry for insect shells in which they could heat water, and with Henry's help he made three hammocks from spider's web. Olsen worked in a purposeful way at these tasks, his hands deftly weaving and knotting the hammocks. Henry watched the hands; they moved together like two brown creatures. They were thick and strong but dextrous, like those of a sculptor or a virtuoso pianist, and they seemed to have a life of their own. Even when he stood inactive with his arms loosely at his sides, they seemed eager to catch at and move and shape things.

Dilke removed the transmitter from its case, tightened every screw in sight and finally got through to Price. Shouting through a sea of static he complained about not being told of Olsen's revised arrival date, then discovered that head office had tried but failed to make radio contact. He suggested that if he was unable to improve the transmitter's performance he would leave it at the collecting point to be picked up and repaired. Price replied that he would prefer to send a new and better radio.

The three men had now settled down together; Olsen finished his organization of their living quarters and was eager to go hunting with the new bow.

Dilke explained his plans. He wished to produce a survival manual, and by combining Henry's knowledge and Bill's hunting experience he meant to list food resources and classify insects in terms of their danger to microman. They set out on a series of exploratory expeditions; sometimes they went together, sometimes in pairs and occasionally Olsen went alone. The new bow was a formidable weapon though its accuracy was still not perfect,

and they made a third bow so that each man was armed.
Each evening, after a day spent in the plantations and
forests of the allotment, they would return and busy themselves in their own ways: Dilke wrestled with the radio,
Henry listed seeds and fruit and insects in order of
edibility and palatability, Bill Olsen was absorbed in his
plans for a super crossbow. He decided that accuracy with
a do-it-yourself bow using secondhand bolts was impossible and he worked on drawings of a metal weapon to
be made to his specification. The table of relative speed
which Henry had drawn on the thick brass door was
soon overdrawn with Bill Olsen's scribbles and diagrams
of crossbow mechanism.

Olsen had discovered something that French crossbow
men had learnt centuries before when faced by the English
longbow; that the crossbow was enormously powerful but
dangerously slow to load. Olsen devised a twentieth-century crossbow: powerful, accurate and quick-loading.

His final design, sketched over a photograph of a
fourteenth-century Milanese bow, was part crossbow, part
lever-action Winchester, part telescopic hunting rifle, part
Gatling gun. He specified that it should be made from
anodized aluminium, matt olive-green. The bolts were to
be tubes as thick as his thumb with a slug of lead in one
end and a screw cap sealing the other; part of the kit was
a syringe with the capacity to fill a single bolt with venom.

Dilke made a combined shopping list.

For himself: A new radio telephone.

A guide and repair manual for the telephone.

A kit of radio repair tools.

For Scott-Milne: A first-aid outfit.

A semaphore mirror.

Writing materials.

Microfilmed copies of:—

European Flora & Fungi—Hutchin-
son.

An Encyclopaedia of Arthropods—
Pendennis.

A set of logarithmic tables.

Slide rule.

                    Camera.
                    Electric torch.
For Bill Olsen: Three crossbow kits as specified.
                    Axe.
                    Machete.
                    Auger.
                    Range of metal files.
                    Wood saw.
                    Hacksaw.
                    Portable light alloy vice.
                    Block and tackle.
                    1,000 mm. of 0.005 mm. galvanized
                    wire.
Dilke checked the list over and read it into the temperamental transmitter and was given a provisional delivery date.

That evening they took a stroll to the shed threshold to look out over the country which glowed in the light of the setting sun. This walk had become something of a ritual, it was a time for reviewing the day's events and for planning tomorrow's programme. 'I want you both to make a marksman's chart to show where to shoot insects, particularly where to hit and kill the dangerous ones when they're attacking. Will you make a short list tonight, Henry, of likely insects? Ants, wasp, centipedes, that sort of thing, and tomorrow you can set off and start some field studies . . .'

Bill Olsen interrupted him by laying a silencing hand on his arm and pointing to a movement on the ground below the wooden threshold.

The movement was in a small depression beside the track along which they usually walked when leaving the shed. As they watched, the depression became deeper and wider, as if the earth was being sucked down from below.

'Ant lion,' breathed Henry. 'Lava of the myrmeleontid fly. I've seen them in Middle Europe and as far north as Finland but they're new here. They'll suck you dry and spit out the bones!' The depression had widened into a crater twenty millimetres across.

'I'll start with that bastard. I'll bring along a bow and winkle him out in the morning,' said Bill Olsen. 'I don't like him next to the track like that.'

They had an early night and Olsen set off at dawn. They saw him shoot a young cockroach on his way and he vanished under the door with his bow under an arm, a machete at his waist and the 'roach on his shoulder.

Thirty minutes later, when they were preparing breakfast, there came a shout from the floor below and a tug on the rope as a signal to haul it up. It took the strength of both men to lift the heavy object. They sweated at their task till over the edge of the platform came the severed head of an ant lion: a monstrous head covered in heavy plating which was streaked with green fluid from the cut neck, the fringed mouth parts used to suck out the juices of its victims protruded from below the catching jaws of the creature. This was the first time Dilke had seen this terror of the ant world so closely and clearly. The jaws were enormous; spread like two horns as wide as a man's outstretched arms. Terrifying in their destructive power, thick as a man's waist near the head, they tapered to pointed tips and were armed along their inner edges with spikes. The end of a crossbow bolt stuck out of one of its eyes.

'Isn't he a beauty!' shouted Bill Olsen as he climbed on to the platform. 'Where shall we put him?'

'Over the mantelpiece,' said Dilke drily.

'Good idea, Mat,' cried Olsen and he hammered a bar into a crevice above the platform fire and lashed the trophy to it. Both men watched him ironically; he stood back to admire the great head: 'How's that . . . is it straight, Henry?'

'It's fine, as long as it doesn't drip into my porridge,' said Henry.

They breakfasted and Henry and Olsen set off for a day's hunting to collect data for the marksman's chart. They left through a side exit and as they walked out of the shadow of the hut they came upon a mob of cicadas scattered through a forest of rye grass. The noise was ear-splitting, each creature giving long burst of song then waiting for a reply. Olsen crept up to a cicada and aimed point blank at its abdomen. The bolt hit the creature when it was in full song. From where he stood Henry saw it pierce the big belly and fly out of the other side. The full deep song stopped abruptly, there was silence for some seconds while the insect stood motionless then it jerked into song again. From its abdomen came a high-pitched chittering sound like an alarm clock on a tin tray. The astonished insect shot into the air and disappeared into the grass jungle.

Bill Olsen grimaced. His second cicada also switched from baritone to castrato and escaped. Olsen turned his head to Henry and mouthed 'Bloody hell!'

Henry took careful aim and hit the nearest singer high up on its back, it fell heavily, kicked a few times and lay still.

Olsen growled, 'He seems to have gone off song . . . what's the trick, Henry?' For answer the younger man took his heavy knife to the dead insect; he hacked off the end of its abdomen, revealing a drum-like cavern—quite empty. He thrust a hand inside and prodded with his finger at a knot of muscle and nerve cords which was attached to the top of the abdomen. 'That's the trick.' He circled a hand in the void of the big belly. 'This is just a sound box—hit him here and you only put a hole in his loudspeaker, Bill. But hit him up there and you destroy a nerve centre.'

'Good. Bloody good. I like that!' Bill grinned. 'Let's get Mat on to this game—but don't tell him where their breadbasket is.' He kicked the severed bowl and it rolled in a wobbling circle, 'We could start a soup kitchen with that . . . or a bath house.'

Weary of the shattering cicada song, they left the grass, crossed a plain and entered a forest of yellow cress where they ate their midday meal and lay back to rest in the shade.

Olsen fell asleep and Henry gazed up at the patches of blue between the green leaves and yellow blossoms. High in the August sky a swarm of winged insects whirled and Henry watched the flash of their wings as they wove flight patterns in the hot summer air. Under the cress the earth was cool and damp. The light, filtering down through the fleshy leaves, was changed to green; the air was still.

Henry turned on his side and looked at his sleeping companion, then closed his eyes.

A crash in the leaves above woke them both. A winged shape tumbled through the roof of leaves and branches and hit the ground before them. It was a big female fly. Perched on her back was a smaller fly, an ardent jockey who had clung to her throughout their fall from the sky. She walked heavily forward for a few steps, folded her shimmering blue wings against her stout green body and crouched down. The men stared at the motionless creatures.

The diminutive piggyback male at last stirred. His trembling antennae caressed the head of the crouching female.

Henry leaned close to Olsen, 'You see the mating of the saphire fly.'

The antennae delicately explored the female's neck but she remained indifferent. His caresses became more insistent. His antennae beat lightly on her shoulders, and at last she acquiesced. Her head lifted, the tip of her tail left the ground and swung slowly from side to side and a valve gaped between the last two segments of her abdomen. Her lover scrambled backwards and grappled her in sexual embrace. Their congress was a long and ecstatic labour rising in a series of climaxes to an ultimate ejaculation. For a while the exhausted lovers lay still, then the female raised her belly from the ground, swollen with now-fertilized egges, and attempted flight—whirring up into the green branches, only to crash back to earth. Her consort was dislodged and she stepped briskly towards the sunlit plain. Taking off, she flew purposefully through the throng of courting insects and vanished into the glare of the sun.

Olsen's attention was fixed on the stricken lover who lay on his side, his body vibrating with little tremors which rose to a crescendo of copulatory jerks. Suddenly the creature got to its feet, staggered sideways and collapsed.

'The job's obviously too big for the poor bastard.'

' "One crowded hour of glorious sex . . ." ' Henry misquoted, 'that's the philosophy of the saphire fly. Born in the morning, gone by night, and the female won't last long after parturition.'

Olsen walked over, placed a palm across the end of a breathing tube and called, 'He's gone all right, I hope it was worth it.'

The big compound eyes reflected them a thousand times in the honeycombed lenses. Above the eyes antennae sprouted like two silk fans and the shimmering membrane of the half-spread wings transmuted the cool forest light into a rainbow of iridescent colours.

'He's rather beautiful, isn't he? It seems a waste, doesn't it, Bill?'

'That's unusually soft-hearted for you, Henry.'

Henry conceded it with a smile.

Olsen unsheathed his machete. 'He *has* got a good head.' He decapitated the insect and they each grasped the base of an antenna and carried it between them out of the forest and across the plain towards home.

Dilke approved of their trophy and they placed it next to the great ant lion head. From the outside the Kremlin began to look like a hunting lodge, inside it was like a ship's forecastle.

Head office rang to say the order could be collected in eight days. The items requested would be at the collecting point—as well as an electronics and weapons expert.

'What do you mean, Major Price?'

'We are sending you a man to operate the radio and to advise you on weapons.'

'I haven't asked for an electronics and weapons expert.'

'The equipment is very sophisticated and this man will be able to service it for you.'

Dilke put down the receiver.

At supper-time Dilke gazed over his bowl of stew at the stack of crossbow bolts in the corner of the platform.

'Henry, what is the difference between nettle and wasp poison?'

'That's an interesting question, Mathew. The strange thing is that though animal and vegetable poison have evolved in different ways they are often remarkably similar. Nettle poison is probably proteinaceous and wasp venom is a protein/enzyme mixture with a high histamine content. Sting for sting, wasp venom is undoubtedly the most virulent, but quantity for quantity—I'm not sure.'

'Let's find out,' said Dilke. 'Bill—I'd like to try wasp venom in the bolts. Will you see if you can get some?'

Bill Olsen nodded, 'I think there's a nest in the honey-suckle. I'll climb up tomorrow and see. And while I'm there I'll go on up and get a view of the country from the roof. Would you like to come, Henry? We'll be back in good time to pick up the stores.'

They started early but they took it easy, stopping fre-quently to rest. At noon they lay on a leaf which over-looked the half-concealed wasp's nest and ate their midday meal. They watched the traffic of wasps roaring in and out of the nest before continuing their climb and they reached the gutter late in the afternoon. The gutter was choked with dust in which fine grass sprouted; they concealed themselves in the thicket and rolled into their blankets for the night.

A shower of dust and rocks woke them. They crawled to the edge of the thicket and looked out. A sparrow was taking its morning dust-bath in the gutter, fluttering its huge wings and pecking at the lice which were dislodged from its feathers. Some of the lice escaped, scuttling past the men for shelter. They had not seen a bird so close before, the formidable horny beak, like the prow of a boat, looked dangerous and they backed into cover and crept away. They climbed on to the corrugated roof and stood in the curve of a shallow valley which sloped gently upwards. They scrambled up the valley side and stood on the ridge; from it they could see the whole roof stretched in iron waves for hundreds of millimetres. Before them the sun rose above the fluted edge of the shed, shining on the cold, dew-wet metal. They walked dreamily towards the ball of light, dazzled by its splendour. After the chill of the night the heat on Henry's body accentuated the coldness of the air and he shivered. They came to the edge of the roof. It was like the edge of the world. The sheer face of the shed fell perpendicularly for two thousand millimetres and spread out below them was the allotment, the garden and the house itself.

They lay in a valley during the morning, sunning themselves. At midday, when the metal had grown uncomfortably hot, they returned down the slope and sheltered from the sun beneath the tangle of honeysuckle which was on the roof. Sand and debris had been washed down the valleys and held by the twisted strands of the plant, lying on the sand were fallen blossoms and the sweet smell of honeysuckle filled the air A trumpet-shaped blossom lay half buried. Henry laid a hand on the end of the great tube where it had parted from the plant stem, the edge was not torn but had a regular notched cut.

'Do you see this, Bill? It's been bitten through by a wasp.' He pointed to the stub from which the blossom had fallen and Olsen saw a dried smear of gum which had oozed from the nectar gland of the plant. 'The regulation way to get at the nectar is along the tunnel of the blossom, pollenizing it in passing (moths stick a long tongue down it for the same purpose), but some wasps don't bother and they take a short cut by chewing off the whole flowerhead and getting at the nectar that way.'

'The little bastards!' grinned Olsen.

'I'll show you.' Henry climbed up into a flowerhead which swayed near the ground.

Olsen put in his head and wrinkled his nose. 'Smells like an Arab whore house.'

Long stamen rods issued from the blossom's interior and Henry cut them out with his machete. Pollen grains were shaken from the stamens and rolled out on to the sand like golden footballs. Olsen climbed up and they bent double to walk into the flower's interior. Henry squatted and plunged his machete into the end wall. A thin, creamy substance ran on to the knife. Olsen reached over Henry's shoulder and with his forefinger transferred some liquid from the blade to his mouth.

'Good, good. Him plenty good, plenty sweet . . .' He rolled his eyes melodramatically, rubbed his belly with a clockwise motion, scooped the edge of his hand along the flat of the knife and licked his palm.

They made camp in the shade and prepared a meal. While looking for fuel in the undergrowth they found and killed a many-legged creature; Henry roasted the legs over the fire. He cut thick slices from a length of stamen, wrapped them in a piece of leaf and buried them—together with a grain of pollen—in the heart of the fire. He twirled the legs on a stick until fluid oozed from them and spluttered in the flames.

They cracked open the legs, split the burnt outer-casing of the ball of pollen and unfolded the leaf containing the steaming cooked slices.

'Meat and two veg,' Olsen spoke with his mouth full. 'My compliments to the chef.'

He finished eating, threw the leg shells and pollen husks into the flames, wiped his greasy hands on the leaf, then lay back and belched.

'That takes care of the washing up . . . now for brandy and cigars. Why the hell didn't I bring some grog, Henry? You should have reminded me.'

They lounged around camp for the rest of the afternoon. As night approached it grew colder and they sat draped in blankets close to the fire.

'I think I'll sleep in the flowerhead, Bill, it should be warm and dry in there.' Henry threw his bedding into the open flower and climbed in after it. He spread the blankets and settled down to sleep.

'You'll smell like a fairy in the morning,' called Olsen, then he built up the fire and lay beside it, his crossbow beside him under the blankets.

They overslept.

Olsen woke beside the grey ashes of the fire, his blankets soaked with dew. He stood and stretched, then pushed at Henry's suspended flower house. It nodded on its stem and Henry climbed stiffly down, yawning audibly. They breakfasted off cold meat and fresh nectar.

Olsen rubbed his nectar-sticky hand together and gestured to a distant sparkle of light through the tangle of creeper. 'That looks like water. How about a wash down?' But Henry was feeling a delayed tiredness from their climb to the roof and he returned to the flower for an after-breakfast rest.

Olsen spread his blankets in the sun then shouldered his bow and walked under the creeper towards the glint of water. He climbed down into the grass-filled gutter and

travelled through the thicket till he came out to a narrow
beach.

Water filled the gutter for as far as he could see. He
knelt at its edge and took some in his supped hands and
raised it to his mouth. The water was bitter; he spat it
out, then scrambled on to the rim of the rusting gutter. He
had expected a lake in which he could bathe but this was
like a disused canal, a yellow film of oxide floated in
patches on its surface and distant dunes blocked its
southern end. A motionless shoal of mosquito larvae was
suspended head down beneath the surface of the water, below them a red, wormlike creature writhed sluggishly.

A sudden movement in the deep, still water startled
Olsen.

A grey shape, trailing a cloud of mud behind it, burst
out of the black sludge in the canal bottom. The water
scorpion took the red worm in its jaws then swooped down
and vanished in a silent explosion of mud. The whole
incident was finished in seconds. Slowly the black cloud
billowed to the surface and the mosquito larvae bobbed
and jostled in the disturbed water.

A pricking sensation crept up the back of Olsen's neck.
He hurried along the edge of the gutter towards the dunes,
climbed them and left the repellant canal behind.

A chain of little pools untainted by chemical deposits
lay in a hollow and he splashed through them until he
found one deep enough to swim in. He left his crossbow
on the bank, waded in and washed, then floated with his
eyes closed.

He lay with arms and legs spread wide and relaxed.
The sun glowed warm through his eyelids. Imperceptibly
his body drifted across the pool, his hand touched the
sandy bank and he woke from his sun-induced coma. He
sat up abruptly, his head went under with a splash and he
struggled to his knees.

The water was quite drinkable, he gulped it down then
waded out, picked up his bow and headed for camp.

The camp was deserted; his blankets still lay around
the ashes of last night's fire. He walked towards the
flower in which Henry had slept. The morning sun shone
through the blossom. 'Lazy young bastard.'

Olsen stopped.

Two dark shapes were discernible through the translucent wall of the flower: a small one at the end of the tube and a big one near its entrance. The larger shape moved stealthily forward.

Olsen fired six bolts into the moving shadow. He fired like a machine, loading and shooting as he ran. At his first shot the thing stopped. At his second, a screeching buzz came from inside the flower. The creature within struggled with frantic violence and the flower jerked wildly. He pumped in the third, fourth and fifth bolts. The fabric bulged and stretched, he crouched beneath the curve of the flower and rammed the nose of the crossbow against it. He could feel the heavy vibrating body within. At his last shot the plant gave a final jerk, a black claw at the end of a bristling leg burst through one of the holes made by the crossbow then the whole mass swayed slowly to a stop.

He looked into the mouth of the flower. A tangle of claws and wings blocked the passage. A drop of venom was slowly expelled from the sting of the dead wasp.

'Henry!' he shouted. There was no reply.

He ran under the flower and cut a V-shaped slit in its pale belly, he pulled the flap down and stood with his head inside the passage.

Henry sat with his knees drawn up and his back to the end of the tunnel. His face was vacant, his wide eyes fixed on those of the insect.

Olsen looked up. Even though the creature was dead, the glittering multi-celled eyes and terrible fangs seen so close made him shudder. He touched Henry's ankle.

"Come on out, lad,' he said gently. 'It's dead now.'

Henry climbed awkwardly through the hole and walked stiffly from the flower. His face was white, his hands were cold. Olsen relit the fire and the younger man lay beside it beneath a blanket.

Olsen squatted quietly by the fire and poked it with a stick. "It reminds me of a trip I made in 'fifty-nine. I took out a Yank after elephant. Nothing would do but elephant! We had the bloody lot: three trucks, a dining tent, canvas baths, a 'fridge, enough Bourbon and Coke to float a battleship.'

Henry smiled wanly.

'On the first night out a leopard came into camp after my dog. The little tyke hid under my bed and I woke up with the leopard on my chest. What with the dog howling, and me and the cat fighting it out, we woke up "Frank Buck". He rolled out of bed, grabbed the first gun that came to hand—luckily it was a small-game shotgun— and let fly in our general direction.'

Bill Olsen fell back, gasping with laughter. 'He blew a hole in the tent and got the dog and me and the cat in one go—the leopard took off with a load of buckshot up his backside and I didn't see Patch for three days.

'My gun bearer did a rough job of sewing on me . . .' he ran a thumb along the puckered scar on his neck and chest '. . . but antibiotics and a case of Old Grand-Dad saw me right.'

Henry laughed noiselessly.

Olsen looked across the fire and saw behind his companion the flower with the stiff leg of the wasp thrust through it. Fluid from the insect's body had gathered in the flower trumpet and was dripping through the hole which had been cut.

He rose briskly. 'We'll shift camp before we have a mob of ants paying respects to your deceased friend.'

Henry collected the blankets, Olsen kicked out the fire and got together the rest of their gear. He handed over Henry's bow. 'Always keep it handy.' It was a rebuke.

They crossed several valleys and made a second camp. While Henry built a fire Olsen left him, ostensibly to hunt for supper. In fact, he returned to the old camp and climbed into the open flower. The black wasp was as full of arrows as a Christian martyr. He retrieved and filled them from its poison sac, forcing venom through the sting by pressing on its tail. He emptied nettle poison from the bolts he carried and refilled them with venom. The blankets were torn, ripped by the brute's struggles; he pulled one out but it was foul with blood and excrement and he flung it back.

In Olsen's absence, Henry had made a shelter under the curve of a fallen leaf, excluding the passage of air along one side by digging a trench into which the edge of the leaf sank. A fire burned at the hovel's entrance, lighting and warming its interior.

They ate, then shared out the depleted blankets and slept.

Next day they lay again in a valley overlooking the garden. Olsen was on his belly, squinting over the edge of the roof, searching for tracks in the sunny landscape below.

Henry lay back, his eyes closed. ' "Something in the insect seems to be alien to the habits, morals and psychology of this world, as if it has come from some other planet, more monstrous, more energetic, more insensate, more atrocious, more infernal than our own." ' He paused. 'Yesterday, I really knew what Maeterlinck meant by that. The wasp you killed has an extraordinary way of reproducing itself. It builds a spherical jug of mud with a hole in the top. It finds a victim, paralyses it with a sting then drops it into the jug. When the bottom of the jug is filled with victims, it lays an egg which it suspends inside the jug on a thread, then it seals the entrance. When the egg hatches the grub drops on to the paralysed victims and eats them alive.'

'Disgusting!' said Olsen.

'Yet you must admire the incredible ingenuity," defended Henry.

'Bloody clever! I'll kill every one I come across,' growled Olsen. He rolled over and stared at the sky. 'There *is* something which seems miraculous to me: how they made us this size.'

'To neolithic man a man on a bicycle would have been a miracle,' said Henry.

'Do *you* know how it's done?'

'Probably with hormones. I talked to the doctor in charge, he was pretty secretive, but he dropped a hint. There are probably lots of ways it can be done; I think hormones are pretty crude and they may be researching other methods.'

'What other methods?'

Henry smiled. 'Do you want a lecture?'

'We've got all day and I can always sleep through it.'

'A miracle would be the *neatest* way—you'd need a special dispensation. Or it could be mind over matter,

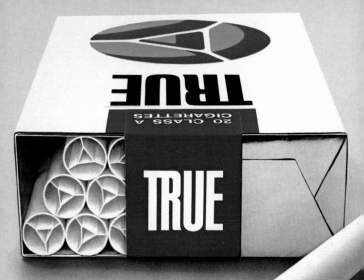

Latest U.S. Government
tests of all cigarettes
show True is
lower in both
tar and nicotine
than 98% of all other
cigarettes sold.

Think about it.
Shouldn't your next cigarette be True?

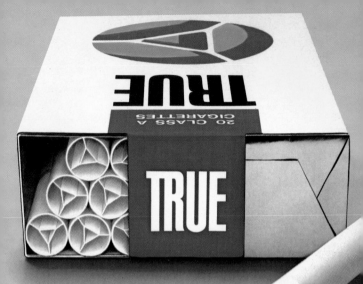

Latest U.S. Government
tests of all menthol
cigarettes show
True is lower
in both tar and
nicotine than 98% of
all other menthols sold.

Think about it.
Shouldn't your next cigarette be True?

like walking on the waters, or on hot coals. Mind over matter—think small and you'll be small.'

'I thought you were being serious.'

'All right, Bill. Let's look at it this way—The problem: how to make a man smaller.

'Here's an analogy: how to make a house smaller. First of all you could do it by subtraction—by deleting the less essential parts; garage, conservatory, bathroom, for instance. Or by reducing the number of bricks, thus making each part of the house smaller.

'Or you could use *contraction*—reduce the size of the bricks, thus scaling down the whole house.'

'To hell with analogies.'

'The crudest form of subtraction would be to reduce the volume of a man surgically. Cut out his spare parts. He could manage with one lung and one kidney—a lot of people live without duplicate organs . . .'

'Balls?' suggested Olsen.

Henry smiled. 'A girl in America who was excessively tall had twelve inches of bone removed from her legs. You'd have to repackage the body to get any benefit, of course, no point in leaving a vacuum. You could have a more compact trunk; perhaps move the brain into the lung cavity. Leave a little stub on the shoulders with a cluster of sense organs.'

'You have got some gruesome ideas, Henry.'

'However, this crude surgical subtraction would not make much difference in size, and you'd have a pretty utilitarian sort of chap at the end of it. But if you subtract from the number of body cells, reducing them to the minimum number needed by the body to function, that could make a big difference. A 50 per cent reduction in cells would reduce a man's volume by the same percentage—like reducing the number of bricks in a house.'

'But we're *three hundred* times smaller.'

'That's why *contraction* is the solution. The whole structure must be reduced in proportion. And I'll bet a lot of specialists are working on it now: chemists, biologists, geneticists, physicists, astronomers . . .'

' Astronomers!'

Henry sat up and thoughtfully lobbed a pebble up the side of the valley. It rattled up the curve then returned to his hand. 'The biggest radio telescopes have revealed Black Stars—quasars—incredibly concentrated universes, so dense that they emit no light; their gravity has condensed billions of tons of matter into the size of this . . .' Henry dropped the pebble on to Bill Olsen's chest '. . . an astronaut coming within a quasar's influence might conceivably be condensed in size; or squashed flat! Another sort of space/time juggling would be to convert a man's mass into energy—Einstein says it can be done—which would give you a man in the form of electromagnetic waves. Reduce the amplitude of the waves, then re-convert the waves to mass and you'd have a smaller man.'

Olsen smiled sceptically.

'Well, perhaps all that is a bit speculative; but one thing is certain, some part of a creature's mechanism must govern its final size—isolate that part and you may have the means of controlling size. What causes the difference between midgets and giants? Or pigmies and Watusies? Or fleas and elephants? I think the stuff they dosed us with was probably a concentrate of some glandular substance which makes midgets and pigmies and fleas small.

'But a more sophisticated way of miniaturizing would probably be to muck about with D.N.A.—deoxyribonucleic acid.

'D.N.A. holds the mystery of the transmission of characteristics from parents to children.' Henry held up his hands, the curved palms and fingers facing. 'It consists of two rods, one inherited from your father, the other from your mother. They act as a sort of blueprint for your basic physical and mental make-up and every cell in your body has a pair. Along the length of each rod are countless nodules, and each nodule controls some part of you: the size of your head, the colour of your eyes, your blood type, you proclivity to live a long or short time.

'*One* of these tiny control points must regulate growth.' He frowned with concentration. 'This is the area which I would explore. The tiniest creatures must also have their blueprints. If one could exchange an insect's growth-control nodule with a man's perhaps by micro-surgery at the moment of conception—then that man should inherit the size natural to the insect . . .'

'And a right little monster you might get.'

Henry turned in surprise at the disapproval in Olsen's voice. 'Carry on, Henry, I'm fascinated.'

'Alternatively, if one had lots of time one could *breed* tiny people (enormous variation in size is possible with selective breeding: look at the difference between a St Bernard and a Chihuahua). Breeding combined with diet might work very well. But it would take an eternity . . .' Henry brooded over this '. . . unless the metabolic rate increased as the generations grew smaller . . . fruit flies have such a short life cycle that you get fifty generations in a year. But what would be the use of a man who passed from childhood to senility in a week?' Henry lay back and stared interrogatingly at a small white cloud which hung in the otherwise empty sky. 'We might monkey about with his genes, and increase his life span once we'd got him down to size?' He waited hopefully, as if for an affirmation.

Olsen watched him.

Now he lay, kneading his lower lip between thumb and finger, silently pursuing the problems of miniaturization along more and more complex labyrinths of theory. 'Yes,' he said softly, 'that might work . . .'

Olsen raised himself on an elbow, the pebble slid off his chest on to the roof, and Henry glanced quickly up.

'You're very well up on all this medical stuff, Henry.'

'A mine of useless information,' smiled Henry. 'My Uncle George is a bio-chemist.'

Olsen sent the pebble bouncing down the valley towards the distant camp. 'We'de better be getting back. Come on, lad, let's have the chef's special and an early night—we've got a long day tomorrow. It will be harder going down than climbing up.'

Bill Olsen was right. It took them two more hours to descend to the ground than it had taken to climb to the roof. They started in the dim light of early morning, passed the great wasps' nest of baked clay at midday and by the time they had reached the ground and climbed to the Kremlin platform Henry was ready for bed.

Dilke had retired to his hammock. Olsen entered noisily and reported that it smelled like a bloody flower shop up on the roof. They celebrated the success of the expedition with the last of the whisky.

When Henry and Dilke woke in the morning Bill Olsen had got the fire blazing and was out on the platform sawing two intersecting grooves in the lead crowns of his crossbow bolts.

'We'll see some fun today, my old son,' he greeted Henry.

After breakfast they prepared for the day's hunting, then descended to the shed floor and headed for the stream near the water butt.

Mist lay on the water hole and they waited for the first insects to arrive. The sun had not yet risen and their breath steamed into the still air; Henry shivered.

The first grasshoppers rattled out of the plantation and bent their heads to drink. Henry and Dilke picked out two insects and dropped them; the two hoppers died instantly and the rest of the mob panicked, shooting at all angles into the air.

'Let's find something bigger,' growled Olsen.

They came on a water-beetle round a curve in the stream. It stood in the shallows munching a green scum of algae which clung to the bankside.

Olsen shot deliberately into its armoured side.

It dropped into the water and lay at the centre of receding ripples. The ripples died away, leaving the beetle and its motionless mirror image.

'I'll show you something, Henry,' Bill said.

He led them to the beetle and the three men strained to turn the big carcase on to its back; they stood side by side and lifted in unison; the beast went over with a sucking, squelching sound and Olsen opened up its mud-stained belly with his machete.

The effect of the shot had been explosive. The grooved lead slug had fragmented; the tube had burst inside the body—shooting venom deep into the tissues. Olsen recovered the fragments of slug and displayed them on his palm, turning them this way and that with his thumb. 'The Bill Olsen Wasp Venom Dum Dum!' he laughed. Patent applied for . . . What shall we call them, W.V.D.D.s or just B.O.s?' He dropped the flattened quarters into the muddy water. 'Let's find something bigger.'

They walked into the plantation.

A heavy dew was vapourizing in the mid-morning sun, drifting down the slopes toward them in a thin mist. On the brow of the hill they came on to the track which led north to the house. At a point where the plantation ended a promontory of green chickweed straggled out into the open desert. The hunters walked under the cover of the weed and rested in the shade of its round fleshy leaves.

They lay and squinted across the glaring sunlit plain. Far away and coming towards them moved a domed brown shape. The sun flashed from its polished surface and as it approached they saw it was a huge insect.

'What the hell is it?' asked Olsen.

Henry shaded his eyes, 'Stag beetle,' he said.

It came at a steady pace, veering neither to right nor left, leaving a churned-up double track in the flat plain, surmounting small clods and crawling straight across any ant lion craters which were in its path.

It was flanked by a half dozen scavenger ants. As the beetle drew nearer, the ants darted ahead and raced past the concealed men into the plantation.

The beetle was an old male, huge, battered and powerful. One of its six legs was lame, adding a discordant squeak to the measured clanking of the other five. It hissed and wheezed like a steam engine and at thirty paces they could clearly see the swivelling eyes beneath its jutting horns. The great hulk was protected by armour-plating which was dented and scarred by past battles.

Dilke knelt and brought his bow slowly to his shoulder. 'Leave him, Mat! I want him.' Olsen stepped into the sun. He waited till the towering creature was abreast of him. He waited till the nearest foreleg lay back, revealing the underpart of its thorax—then he pressed the trigger. The bolt zapped into the lightly armoured belly and vanished. The hissing stopped.

The beetle teetered forward, then the front legs stiffened and snapped straight, the back legs collapsed and the beast sat down with a noise like a ton of scrap iron being dumped. The ground shook; there was silence.

They stared at the thing for a minute.

A shimmering blue fly zoomed down, skidded in the loose sand and turned to face the motionless beetle, then it ran on twinkling legs towards it. Bill Olsen said quietly, almost to himself, 'You beauty!'

They set off home; from halfway up the hill they looked back. At the end of the avenue of carrots they could see the dead beetle. It sat propped up at an angle, its long horns aimed at the sky—like a sculptured howitzer cast in bronze: Memorial to the Glorious Dead.

Two more buzzing dots spiralled down and the three men turned and walked south.

It was late when they reached home and retired to their hammocks.

'I feel like a hot bath and a damn good booze-up!' Bill Olsen exclaimed.

'You'll have to wait a long time for either, Bill,' said Dilke.

'You never know your luck, Mat,' Olsen winked across at Henry, pushed at the wall with his foot and sang in Afrikaans to the rhythm of his swinging.

Dilke transferred his gaze from the flickering light on the chamber ceiling to Olsen. 'You're in very high spirits, Bill. What're you up to?'

'You never know your luck, Mat,' Olsen repeated. 'What time are we collecting the mechanical wonder-boy tomorrow? Let's make an early start.'

'Do *you* know what he's up to, Henry?'

Henry shook his head.

4

They hurried off next morning, eager to pick up the stores, although Dilke was a little subdued by the thought of the new man who had been wished on him.

On one of his hunting trips Olsen had found a disused ant track which went most of the way from the hut to the house and they made fast time along it, reaching the gap between the French windows before noon. The potted plant was dead; its leaves, like black, withered hands, lay on the floor and they walked under them and climbed the cable to the window seat.

A man sat on a box, dressed in air-force blue.

He sat with his head in his hands, among a pile of bags, boxes and packing cases like a traveller who has spent all night on a railway platform.

Olsen gave his Bantu call and the man jumped up, knocked over the box on which he had been sitting and stared at the approaching figures.

All three were tanned and covered in trail dirt; armed with bows and knives—like savages.

The man in blue had a strained white face; he looked uncertain, as though unable to decide whether to make a run for it or raise a white flag. Dilke walked up and shook his hand.

'This is Bill Olsen . . . Henry Scott-Milne . . . I am Mathew Dilke . . .'

He waited for the man's name.

There was a pause. '00.25/4, Sergeant Charles Wallis, sir,' he swallowed.

All three eyed him solemnly, his eyes behind his spectacles flickered from one face to the other, desperately avoiding their nakedness. As the silence lengthened a slight flush colored his white face and suddenly he looked down and fumbled at the button of a patch pocket. He produced an official envelope and gave it to Dilke. 'This is from Major Price, sir.'

Dilke opened it and while he read Bill Olsen moved silently up to Sergeant Wallis and stood almost touching him. Through the dust from the trail Olsen's body still showed the shirt, shorts and sandals patterns, the once-white areas were now coffee brown against the deeper mahogany red; he looked as if he was on his way to a corroboree. He reached out a hand and put his finger on a moulded button. Wallis flinched nervously. The brown hand took a sleeve between finger and thumb and silently rubbed at its texture; then he turned abruptly and walked away to the corner of the window and passed behind the curtain.

'Hang on to this.' Dilke returned the letter and started to inspect the equipment. Henry was searching the boxes for his camera and slide rule. Dilke stood before a big packing case marked THIS WAY UP.

'What the hell is this?' he asked.

'That was my idea, sir.' Wallis stepped forward anxiously. 'It's an electric motor; I thought we could run a drill from it and maybe other equipment.'

'And what will you power it with?'

'We could have a battery delivered if we can't use the mains.' Under the interrogation Wallis showed a hint of stubbornness.

'We are half a day's march from here, how do you think we're going to get it there? It must weigh a ton.'

Wallis looked at the floor. 'I could *dismantle* it, sir.'

Dilke turned his back. 'Where the hell has Bill got to?' As he spoke Olsen came from behind the curtain and approached them, grinning. He had a polythene demijohn in each hand and another tucked under one arm.

Dilke's expression changed; he laughed and took the proferred bottle. 'One apiece,' said Olsen, putting down the third next to Henry. 'Oh! Sorry, Sergeant. I was forgetting you. Here, have a swig, you look done in.'

Charles Wallis politely refused the drink, then sat down on his box. They began methodically to unpack the equipment and lay it out in a row. The new crossbows were packed together head to tail, each one in an oiled wrapping, and the men undid their parcels as if it were Christmas morning. The bows gleamed a dull, olive-green; the tensioning levers worked fast and the revolving racks, made to hold six bolts, clicked smoothly round. Olsen had ordered a number of solid bolts in addition to the tubes and he loaded the chambers of his bow and shot them off rapidly into the wooden frame of the window. They flew fast and straight, and formed a vertical line with a hand's width between each bolt. Olsen whooped and ran to retrieve them.

Dilke was cheered by the excellence of the equipment and by the whisky. He turned to speak to the new recruit. Sergeant Wallis was sitting on the box, his cap folded and tucked under his tunic epaulette, the flap of his breast pocket unbuttoned and his brilliantined hair in disarray. He sat with his clasped hands between his knees and stared through the window. For a weapons expert he showed surprisingly little interest in the crossbows and it occurred to Dilke, for the first time, that the man's pallor might be caused by illness and not be just a sign of a sedentary life.

When Dilke spoke the sergeant stood up.

'Are you feeling all right?'

'I feel tired, sir, and a bit sick, sir.'

Dilke sat on a box facing the man and motioned him to sit down.

'Look, Sergeant, you can forget the "sir" bit while you're here. This isn't a time for the formality of rank and all that nonsense. My name is Mathew—what are you usually called?'

'Charlie, sir.'

Dilke saw that Charlie used "sir" the way Olsen used "bloody"—unconsciously.

'Well, Charlie, we have a pretty good hike back to our base and I want to take as much of this gear as we can, so we won't be travelling very fast—do you feel well enough to start now?'

'Yes, sir,' Charlie realized he had used The Word and he looked down with an embarrassed smile.

Henry joined them, he held a slide rule and its case and spoke with unusual vehemence. 'Mathew. They haven't sent the camera.'

Dilke made a sympathetic face but before he could speak Sergeant Wallis said, 'Oh, yes, sir, they said that that was difficult. The technical people are still working on it. I think it's the optics that are holding them up.'

'What about your glasses?' Henry asked sharply.

Wallis glanced apprehensively at Dilke. 'But they need compound lenses for cameras. I think they're trying plastics instead of glass.'

'Damn!' Henry slapped the rule into its case.

Dilke smiled consolingly then began briskly to organize things. They discussed which equipment they would take on their first trip: the weapons, the radio telephone, the electric torch, the axe and a length cut from the big coil of wire.

Dilke reported the safe arrival of the equipment to Department 7A, then they loaded up and started the journey. A fourth bow had been sent for Charlie Wallis and each man carried a cross bow kit. Dilke shouldered the radio phone and the other items were shared out. Charlie hesitantly descended the swaying wire, his boots slipping on the smooth cable, and when they left the house and started the ascent of the rockery slopes he made hard work of the long climb. They rested frequently and finally Dilke took from him the quiver of bolts, leaving him with a token crossbow to carry.

To Charlie Wallis the journey was a nightmare. He was stifled by the heat and his joints ached with his efforts to keep up with the party. He walked in third place followed by Bill Olsen; as the hours passed his breathing quickened and he walked with his head down, stepping out doggedly through a sea of exhaustion. All his efforts were concentrated on putting one foot before the other; he hardly registered the incongruity of the bus in Park Lane and when they finally reached the allotment shed patches of sweat blackened his uniform and his feet were blistered and raw.

Dilke looked anxiously at the grey-faced stumbling man

and wondered how he would manage the climb to the ledge. When they reached the foot of the box Wallis looked up at its towering face and he turned a shade paler. They rested for ten minutes; Dilke and the others talked cheerfully amongst themselves and to the withdrawn sergeant.

'We'd better get going, lads, before it gets too dark to see. Do you feel up to it, Charlie?'

Charlie nodded.

Dilke pointed out the route up the box side, tracing in the air with his hand the ledges and crevices up which they must climb; and then with himself in the lead and with Wallis, Henry and Bill Olsen following they began to climb. When they reached the ledge it was quite dark and the glow from the fire greeted Dilke as his head came above the platform ledge. He turned and dragged the exhausted Wallis up and, while Henry made up the fire and Bill Olsen prepared supper, Dilke showed Charlie the quarters. Indicating the fourth hammock Dilke urged him to climb in and later they brought him his food and drink. Charlie drank a little water, swallowed a few mouthfuls of vegetable stew, then lay back and stared at the ceiling. The three men sat in the chamber talking rather quietly together as if in a sick room, glancing occasionally at the still figure in the hammock. At last he closed his eyes and they heard him breathing more regularly as he slept. They were awakened in the night by a shout.

'No. Yes. No. Yes. No. Yes.'

Dilke shone the torch on Wallis's hammock. The man's eyes were closed, his jaw muscles worked convulsively, they could hear his teeth grinding. Dilke switched off the torch.

5

When the early light filtered in, Dilke awoke. Charlie stood just inside the chamber door looking out into the huge gloomy cavern of the shed, as if afraid to leave the chamber. Dilke swung out of his hammock and silently approached.

'Good morning, Charlie, how have you slept?'

Sergeant Wallis quickly turned his head, his eyes were wide, tears lay on his cheeks.

Dilke was embarrassed and he stepped past the man on to the platform. Wallis wiped his cheeks with the palms of his hands and followed Dilke outside. 'I'm sorry if I've been any trouble, sir. I don't know what's wrong with me. I didn't sleep too well. Maybe it's the drugs.' Wallis had said what Dilke had suspected from the moment he had seen him seated on his box staring out at the garden.

'I expect it's because of the long march from the house and the climb at the end of it. Let's get some breakfast going, you'll feel better after that; and you'd better take it easy today and maybe get some more sleep. Tomorrow we'll have a look at the radio phone, I'd like you to explain it to me.'

Wallis cheered up a little. He sat by the fire and fed it from the wood pile. Later, when Henry and Bill came out, stretching and yawning, he returned their 'good mornings' quite brightly. He remained behind when they went for a swim and when they returned he had set up the radio in a corner of the chamber and he offered to give lessons on its operation. His mood of cheerfulness lasted till the afternoon, when he became lethargic and silent. He retired early and they heard him tossing restlessly during the night.

Charles Wallis was clearly a sick man. It was plain that this new world frightened him; he was afraid to descend to the floor of the shed and he watched the busy insect life with fascinated apprehension.

Dilke decided that Charlie could be most useful as fulltime radio operator and keeper of the sacred flame, allowing the others to concentrate on fact-finding and fieldwork.

The next day they journeyed to the house and returned with the rest of the gear, leaving only the motor and a couple of bottles in Olsen's secret cache.

Charlie had supper ready when they returned and the following morning he was up early and prepared breakfast; he was generally happier, but his mood of melancholy sometimes returned. He was most animated when describing the workings of the radio and he gave Dilke a course on its function and operation. They sat side by side in the chamber with the instrument and a chart of its controls before them. Charlie detailed each dial, knob and button and then turned the radio on its face and revealed its interior. Dilke was impressed by its complexity and fine finish: it was a maze of printed circuits and minutely soldered joints.

'Extraordinary! How have they done it, Charlie? This is a hundred times better than my old set.'

Charlie's eyes glowed with enthusiasm.

'They've done it in stages. Not even a Japanese bead stringer could work to the fine tolerance necessary for this size of radio, and the same goes for these tools,' he held up a wallet containing screwdrivers and pliers and a soldering kit.

'They've done it in three stages. There are three teams of engineers and craftsmen: the first lot are reduced to about one foot high—and they have made the smallest machine tools and bench instruments they can. The second lot are about two inches high and they use these tools and tiny instruments to make even smaller ones. And finally the third and smallest team—about half an inch high—have made this radio and your crossbows and Henry's

slide rule and . . .' the thought came to him . . . 'my
uniform and boots and things!'

Charlie beamed.

'I wouldn't change places with them,' said Dilke.

'Sir?' asked Charlie.

'What happens to them later? Sooner or later we'll be
making our own stuff, then they'll be on the shelf.'

'Oh, no,' said Charlie. 'They can join us then. When
the intermediate stages are no longer needed their miniaturizing will be completed.'

'Now that *is* clever.'

Dilke sat back and shared Charlie's joy at the elegance
of the concept.

'And the labs are working on DeMin, Sir.'

'*DeMin?*'

'Deminiaturizing. The technocrats have been promised
they may be able to go back . . .' Charlie was disconcerted
by the intensity of Dilke's gaze . . . 'back to their proper
size.'

'Who told you that?'

'A stage-three engineer, sir.'

'An escape route,' Dilke reflected. 'It sounds plausible.
And might help recruitment.'

He called Henry over.

Henry was sceptical about DeMin. 'I haven't heard of
it. It must be an extremely *long* business and might take
years. It would be an additive process, and putting on
weight is vastly different from taking it off.'

A new routine started. Dilke, Henry and Olsen left each
morning and returned in the evening to supper prepared
by Charlie. Apart from occasional moods of depression
Charlie seemed to have cheerfully accustomed himself to
the role of radio operator and cook/housekeeper. But
Dilke was concerned about the restless nights which he
endured, for his sleeping mind was full of nameless
terrors. More disturbing was a deterioration in Charlie's
health; his breathing became asthmatic and he developed
an ear-ache which finally caused him to give up his telephone duties. To shut out sounds to which he had become
painfully sensitive he wore a clumsy Balaclava helmet
made from several thickness of blanket. His appetite

diminished and one evening he left his supper untouched to go to bed. Stepping towards the open door of the chamber he stumbled and veered sideways across the platform. Before he could reach the edge and fall Bill Olsen rose swiftly from his place by the fire and took his arm. 'Look out, Charlie, you'll take off!' He led him away and Dilke, who had finished eating, took him in to bed.

Olsen returned to his supper.

'Henry.' He paused thoughtfully between blows on the casing of a baked insect's leg. 'How long a life will miniaturization give us?'

'Why do you ask, Bill?'

'I wondered if size affects how long you can live.' He pointed up to the trophy head which they had taken from the corpse of the spent saphire fly, 'Lover boy didn't last long, did he?'

'Lover boy is a special case,' said Henry. 'It's true that life span is usually related to an organism's size, but there are exceptions: a pike can live for two hundred years while the much larger horse has a life expectancy of only thirty.'

'And what would happen to a bloody *horse* if he were brought down to our size?'

'He should be all right. An animal's life span is usually five times as long as it takes it to reach maturity, the Greeks thought it was eight times but Flourens has revised that.

'Our physio/chemical time-clock was set before we were reduced so we should follow the proper pattern—maturity, times five.'

Henry smiled up at the fly's head mounted on the wall above them, 'Anyway, you aren't subject to such strain as he."

'The chance would be a fine thing!' Bill Olsen split open the leg and dug at the meat within.

The weather was good for several days, but one morning they woke to see an overcast sky through the shed window. The walls of the chamber were wet with condensation and the atmosphere was humid and sticky.

Dilke decided to join in a hunt along the southern boundary of the allotment. They waved to Charlie from

the shed floor and set off due west to a huge forest of
rhubarb on the horizon. The day brightened a little but
by mid-morning blue-black clouds had crept over the horizon and there were a few spots of rain. Insect life was
subdued by the heavy atmosphere; cicadas were silent, the
men looked up and saw that the green-and-black fly had
stopped their normal slow browsing and were quite still,
clustered in herds beneath the leaves.

They had nearly reached the rhubarb forest and Dilke
had almost decided to turn back for home when thunder
growled overhead and the first big raindrops fell. They
could hear the distant roar of approaching rainfall and
they ran together to the shelter of the first rhubarb plant.
The drops thudded into the dust around them, each one
big enough to knock them to the ground.

They reached the shelter of the leaf just as the rain fell
in sheets. They settled themselves at the foot of a huge
stalk and looked out on a landscape obscured by drifting
clouds of rain. Bill Olsen lay on his back and looked up
at the enormous umbrella of the leaf with its ribs arching
away from the main stem like the roof of a Gothic cathe-
dral. The whole canopy trembled with the force of the
falling rain, the noise of its drumming deafened them,
they could feel the great trunk of the vegetable throbbing,
and sheets of water cascaded from the undulating edges of
the leaf.

The rain stopped as if a tap had been turned off, but
the atmosphere remained oppressive, and lightning flickered all round the horizon. Bill Olsen lay a little apart
from Henry and Dilke, the heavy atmosphere started an
ache in his head and he closed his eyes, spanned his forehead with a hand and pressed on his temples with thumb
and forefinger. The air was stifling.

He lay for a minute, conscious of an intense and elec-
trically charged atmosphere. He yawned, removed his
hand from his face and opened his eyes. A few paces
from him stood a huge ant, twelve millimetres long, bright
crimson, like the rhubarb stalk near which he lay. An
intense, whining sound like a dentist's drill came from its
interior. The huge mechanical beast seemed to be under
stress. It stood stiffly, throbbing; its antenna twitched and
jerked, the sound which sent Olsen's teeth on edge fluc-

tuated in volume and suddenly the ant jerked forward several steps then stood still again. Olsen realized that it was either unaware of or cared nothing for his presence, and he slowly edged round the plant to where his companions sat against the rhubarb trunk.

Henry turned his head and was silenced by Olsen's strained face and the curt gesture of his hand. Olsen jerked a thumb behind him and Henry leaned forward and looked over his head. 'By God! *Formica rufa!*' he swore. Fifty millimetres away a second ant, which was similar in every respect to the first, ran forward.

All three men now sat motionless and stared across the forest floor into its dark interior. The shadow was broken in places by light filtering down through gaps and occasionally a sluice of water cascaded down from above, sparkling like silver against the dark leaves.

They all now felt the electric tension in the air and, as they watched, more ants appeared, running forward in short epileptic bursts under the vaults of the leaves, mostly dark silhouettes in the shadows but gleaming ruby-red when they ran through clearings. They moved in one direction, travelling from the interior towards the forest's edge. The men turned and looked outwards to the open plain.

Approaching the rhubarb forest in the same epileptic fashion was an army of huge black ants. The red ant which Olsen had first seen stepped out from the shade of the leaf. It stood on the edge of the plain, twitching and whining, facing the forerunner of the black ants. Suddenly both ants went into reverse, backing stiffly away from each other for a dozen paces; then they sprinted forward and met head on with a crash of armour. Each monster tried to overturn its opponent, their jaws locked on each other's shoulders, their legs straddled. Their struggles took them back and forward, first out on to the plain, then struggling in a cloud of dust under the roof of the plant where the three men crouched. The black ant slowly overpowered its opponent; it shifted the grip of its huge jaws to the foreleg of the red ant, almost severing the limb where it joined the body. With one leg useless the injured ant was forced sideways, its scrabbling feet kicked up clods of earth and air whistled through its breathing tubes. It was crushed to the ground twenty paces from the trunk of the rhubarb, it fell on its side, blowing up dust in spasmodic bursts. Instantly its conqueror transferred its grip and bit at the gap between head and thorax. The teeth of the black ant chewed with a grinding sound, forcing back the red ant's head. The faces of Henry and Dilke twisted with disgust; a crossbow twanged behind them and a bolt vanished into a breathing tube of the victor. It reared up and fell with a crash on its dying victim.

Bill Olsen smiled blandly at his startled companions.

They saw that they were witnesses to a full-scale war.

The plain was covered by a swarming pattern of red and black; some ants fought singly, but sometimes several ants from one army attacked a single opposing ant. The battle continued throughout the afternoon. The men's ears were filled with the sound of collision, of breaking limbs of grinding jaws and of the unnerving electronic screaming. The stench of formic acid lay on the air as the beasts injected it into their opponents and clouds of dust floated across the battle area. The rattle and crash reminded Dilke of tank exercises on Salisbury Plain.

The afternoon passed, the electric storm which had precipitated the war passed away and the sun slanted low, sparkling and gleaming on the grotesque fighting insects. In the late afternoon the fighting reached a frenzied climax and then slowly it grew quieter and the dust-clouds diminished. The black ants were victorious; the red ants retreated into the forest, trailing useless limbs, falling and dying in their tracks. One with a deep head wound crept to the foot of the rhubarb where the men stood and climbed blindly up it. It stopped after a few jerky climbing movements and remained stationary, its body pressed to the trunk, its feet clutching the ribbed column.

Dilke, Bill Olsen and Henry walked slowly out into the field. They were dazed by the immensity and the ferocity of the battle they had seen. The plain was littered with mounds of broken insects piled high like dead cars in a breaker's yard. The vaporized acid stung their eyes and there was a steady drip, drip, dripping sound from within the mounds. The sky was a flaming shepherd's delight lit by the setting sun; the highlights on the metallic armour of the black ants gleamed as red as those on the opposing army. Everything was as red as death. They started their journey home, trotting between the mounds which made jagged silhouettes against the dying light. The leg of an ant, half-buried under a pile of insects, was steadily jerking as if someone had forgotten to switch off its motor. Dilke shot it in the head and the limb slowly extended and relaxed.

There was no moon that night and they returned to the hut at a fast run, trying to reach home before dark because of night predators. But it was dark when they entered the hut, the fire glowed on the high platform.

'Dear mother's kept a candle lit,' quipped Olsen.

The Kremlin had never seemed more safe and welcoming.

A week later Dilke returned home in the early afternoon. The three men had been hunting together but Dilke went on alone leaving Henry and Bill Olsen behind to take a cooling swim. He climbed on to the platform: the fire was out, the door was shut tight. He looked with surprise at the thick brass door shining in the sun, then he pushed it open and stepped inside. At first he could see nothing; the hammocks were empty; the equipment was stacked neatly on the racks which Charlie had made; but there was no sign of Charlie. Then a slow movement from the farthest corner of the room caught his eye. From a wad of blankets lying against the wall, Dilke saw a white hand surreptitiously pulling at the topmost blanket. Charlie had taken blankets from the hammocks and wrapped himself in them from head to foot. Dilke quietly approached the blue cocoon.

'Charlie? Charlie? Are you all right?'

The hand vanished. The cocoon listened.

'Charlie. This is Mathew,' he touched the shoulder of the figure and gently pulled at the blanket which covered the head. The hand came out and helped to pull the cover aside, then Charlie Wallis struggled to a sitting position with his back against the wall.

'Are you all right, Charlie?'

Charlie did not answer, but he smiled. He was not wearing his glasses, his eyes were wide and bird-bright. In recognition of Dilke's presence one side of his face gave a greeting; the cheek rounded out in a curve, the eye half closed, a fan of wrinkles appeared at its corner and the mouth curled upwards.

Charlie smiled with only the right side of his face. The left side was like wax: stiff, white and quite motionless.

Dilke's heart sank.

He looked down at the man's hands. Charlie sat with his weight resting on his right hand, the other lay stiffly on the blanket like the hand of a corpse.

When Dilke raised his eyes Charlie was staring past him; the half-smile was replaced by a grimace of terror, the one good eye was screwed up, the head averted as if to escape a blow in the face. Dilke turned quickly; the sun shone through the open door and the grotesque shadow of the ant lion's head lay on the floor. He lifted the man to a place where he could not see the horned shadow and settled him comfortably.

'How's that, Charlie? What have you been doing? Do you feel like supper?'

The look of fear had been switched off; the expression was alert, birdlike, the head held on one side, as if he could hear but not comprehend.

'Wait till Bill gets back and finds no supper!'

The half-face smiled at Dilke's teasing manner, an infantile chuckle jerked from Charlie's throat.

Dilke heard voices and he met Henry and Olsen on the platform.

'Something's happened since we've been away. Charlie's sick, he's half frightened to death and he's had some sort of stroke. He may not understand, but talk to him in the normal way.' They entered and looked down on him and chatted. Charlie heaved with baby laughter and they responded with smiles.

They returned to the platform to decide what to do.

'I think this must be the drugs,' said Dilke, 'it's sparked off by something which has shocked hell out of him. What do you think it could be, Bill? He had shut himself in when I got here.'

'A fly has been up here.' Olsen walked to the brass door placed his finger on a number of points where the old crossbow drawings and calculations were smudged. 'You can feel the sticky stuff from its feet, and anyway I can smell the dirty bastard. And look, you can see where its wings have blown most of the fire off the platform.'

Dilke decided that Charlie could not safely sleep in a hammock and he set Olsen to making a bed. He got Henry to prepare some food and look after the sick man and he lifted the radio phone out on to the platform and rang up head office.

Only the night operator was on duty. 'Major Price will be here in the morning, sir. Who shall I say called?' Dilke said it was an emergency and that he needed Major Price immediately. The operator said that she could not give private phone numbers. Dilke used some quiet words of vulgar abuse and within an hour Price had rung him back. He listened to Dilke and said he would get advice from the head of the labs and rang off. Henry was spooning soup into the patient's mouth with 50 per cent success and Bill Olsen had dismantled Charlie's storage racks and reassembled them in the shape of a bed. The legs at the foot of the bed were longer to compensate for the slope of the chamber floor and half a dozen gnat's wings gave a spring base for the blankets.

They got Charlie to bed. He lay with his head muffled in his Balaclava, breathing with little gasps of pain, sweat bathing his face and mucus oozing from his nose.

None of them slept well. Charlie tossed restlessly, his eyes shining feverishly in the firelight, and, even when he slept, the sound of his laboured breathing filed the chamber. The men lay awake in their hammocks listening. Dilke looked down from his hammock; Charlie looked like a dying man.

At eight hundred hours Major Price told Dilke that the laboratories were producing an anti-allergy drug. It should be ready within twelve hours and he would let Dilke know when to pick it up.

'Major Price, it will take me a day to collect this drug and get it back here. I can give you clear directions to deliver it on my doorstep.'

Price's reply had a note of official regret.

'I'm afraid my instructions are to deliver at the prescribed place, Captain Dilke.'

'Sergeant Wallis will die if he's not treated quickly.'

'Lord Raglen has instructed that your exact position is not disclosed—even to this office.'

Dilke slammed down the transmission lever and dropped the microphone.

Bill Olsen sat with his legs overhanging the ledge.

'Who is Lord Raglen?'

'*Lord Raglen* is head of M.I.5,' Dilke turned and stalked into the chamber.

Bill Olsen spat between his knees and watched the gob fall, then he lifted his head and smiled down the length of the shed.

They carried out the bed on to the platform. It was a lovely September day; sun shone through the shed window and the scent of honeysuckle drifted through a broken pane and filled the air.

Charlie dozed and rubbed fitfully at his nose and his breath rasped in his throat.

Henry sat at the foot of the bed. 'He's having trouble with smell as well as his other senses.'

'They've made a real cock-up of his treatment,' said Olsen, 'that's for sure.'

At sundown they carried him indoors and at ten o'clock Dilke was informed that the drug was waiting for collection. He went into the chamber. The breathing of the sick man was slower, his features were relaxed, his eyes closed. Dilke spoke quietly to him, 'Charlie. How are you feeling? We're collecting some stuff which will make you feel better. We'll be back soon.' Deep furrows marked the brow and slowly the eyes opened; they were weary but intelligent.

'We won't be long, Charlie. Henry will stay with you.'

'I feel the cold, sir.'

Dilke put a hand on his forehead; the skin was wet and fish cold.

'Keep him covered,' he said to Henry.

Olsen handed Dilke his crossbow and the torch and they clambered over the side of the platform into the dark. They needed the torch until they entered the garden, then the way was bright with moonlight. They moved fast, alternately walking and trotting; the way was familiar and well lit; in three hours they reached the window seat and Dilke swept its length with the torch. Two long chalk marks had been drawn on the wood forming a huge cross; at its intersection Dilke found a bottle. It lay in the powdered chalk, the capsules inside sparkled in the torchlight. Dilke picked it up and they turned and ran, leaving two lines of chalk footprints to the edge of the seat, fading to nothing as they descended the black cable.

In two hours they had reached the carrot plantation and the breeze which came before dawn swayed the carrot tops. They paused halfway up the hill to regain their breaths. The wind subsided, the rustling overhead stopped, then from behind them and to the east of the track there came a curious sound. As it became louder they could distinguish it more clearly as a crash of feet and the rattle of disturbed stones and rubble. They saw flickering movements in the shadows of the plantation. Both men leapt off the track and stood behind the bole of a carrot. The long shape of a centipede suddenly appeared on the track along which they had travelled, its articulated body metallic in the waning moonlight.

The creature paused momentarily—they crouched down —then it crossed the track and ran swiftly on, its battalion of legs swinging rhythmically. The sound of its movements came in fits and starts till it faded and was overlaid by the sound of the returning breeze.

Dilke released a long-held breath and became aware of the heavy beat of his heart. The wind chilled his sweating body. He wiped his nose with a nervous gesture and stared at Olsen's dim features.

'I don't like it, Mat!' Bill Olsen's voice was edgy.

They went quietly on up the hill, keeping in the shadow and looking often behind them. From the crest of the hill they saw before them the looming bulk of the shed, in half an hour they would be home. They stepped on to the track to start the run downhill. On the wind came the pungent smell of centipede. The big square head and the first ten segments of the centipede's body lifted from the shadows at the side of the track. The sight and smell transfixed them. Its glittering eyes looked down on them, the legs of the monster swam in the air, then it dropped with a crash and attacked.

Dilkes switched on the torch and the beam speared it in the eyes, the multi-lenses flashed like cut-glass and the

brute sheared away, its yellow segments flashing by in the
torchlight. A gust of body odour and the smell of carrion
swept over them, Bill Olsen shouted, 'Look out! Hit him!'
The beast had looped round and attacked again.

Olsen shot it in the head and Dilke pumped two bolts
into the racing body. It was more than thirty millimetres
long and the first half went stiffly into the air, the paired
legs racing madly, then it fell and exploded into huge convoluted writhings. Dilke was swept off the track by the
lashing tail and skidded amongst the carrots on his back,
he jumped to his feet and they both raced on towards the
looming hut. Behind them the noise of the dying centipede
faded into the distance. They climbed the Kremlin wall in
the dawn light.

Henry stood on the edge of the platform. 'Charlie's
dead,' he said.

Dilke entered the chamber. The blue blankets had been
thrown off the bed. The dead man lay at attention. He
was dressed in his R.A.F. shirt, his naked legs stiff, his
bruised feet together. Dilke sat down on the edge of the
bed. The mattress groaned, intensifying the silence; the
man who had laboured so noisily for breath lay still. He
looked faintly supercilious, as if he had private thoughts
which he would not share.

Dilke breathed in deeply and exhaled wearily; he took
the small bottle of green two-tone capsules between thumb
and forefinger and stood it deliberately on the edge of the
bed frame, then got slowly to his feet and left the chamber.

They buried Charlie in the afternoon. They carried him
up on to the roof of the box then lowered him on a rope
down the side which leaned inwards to the ground. The
body was trussed in a blanket and it spun sluggishly in the
air as Dilke paid out the rope. Olsen waited below and
took it across his shoulders when it touched the ground.
They followed him down the length of the shed and under
the door. It was a blustery day with fractious changes of
sun and cloud. Olsen stepped over the edge of the vacant
ant lion crater and carried the body in a sliding walk down
to the bottom of the hole. He straddled the body and dug
with his hands at the fine rubble and the sloping surface
of the crater slid down and covered the corpse. Olsen

struggled up to his companions on the rim of the crater, the wind caught at the disturbed dust and spun it out of the hole and into their eyes. They stood and looked down; then, almost absentmindedly, Bill Olsen raised his cross-bow with one hand and fired it. The wind, blowing across the front of the shed, caught the bolt and carried it side-ways into the garden. It fell away and vanished into the carrot tops.

The radio call rattled as they climbed the Kremlin wall to the ledge. It stopped before they could answer it and Dilke raised his eyebrows at the lateness of the call. Then he rang head office.

Major Price was rather testy; he had been ringing for an hour. He had a message from on high; they were to be picked up the following day at noon and were to go on a mission. They were to bring Wallis with them.

'Sergeant Wallis died last night, Major Price.'

Price expressed his regrets.

'Bring only your weapons, Captain Dilke, all the other equipment will be supplied. The transporter will be on the window seat at twelve hundred hours. Lord Raglen will brief you.'

'What's this all about? How long will the mission take?'

'I'm afraid I can tell you no more, Captain Dilke. Lord Raglen will be speaking to you.'

'We have done a lot of work on a survival manual, it's not yet finished but you'd better have what we've done.'

'Don't worry about that now, Captain, this is more important.'

'Thank you, Major Price.'

'When you get aboard the transporter you can contact me on the radio you'll find there.'

'*Thank* you, Major Price.'

PART THREE

1

On the way to the rendezvous they came to where Dilke and Olsen had been attacked by the centipede. A trail of kicked-up earth led off the track into the grove. Henry was curious, and they followed it; in its agony the wounded beast had ripped up small plants and bitten chunks out of the tall carrots. A whiff of putrefaction came to them on the wind and at a little distance they saw the centipede lying in the shadows, twisted round the trunks of the carrots. Its head and most of its body was swollen with corpse gas; but a section had collapsed; a dozen meat ants had made a way into the long tunnel of its body and were burrowing into it like pigmies into a dead elephant. The ants were preoccupied with their mining, but the men remained at a distance and after a while they moved silently away.

The silver sphere in the middle of the window seat shone in the midday sun. It was as big as a tennis ball and from the entrance at its base came a deep hum. They entered the door, climbed a ramp and came up on to the floor. The inside of the transporter was almost filled by a gyroscope; its central column five millimetres thick, its heavy flywheel a spinning blur. The ends of the column turned in bearings in the floor and ceiling. A circular couch went round the perimeter of the chamber, the floor was carpeted in red. A radio transmitter lay on the couch and Dilke told Price that they were aboard.

After half an hour they felt a lurch as the container was

picked up, then the erratic movements of the car in which
they travelled were translated by the container's gyroscope
into vertical movements. Henry, who was revising his
notes, discovered that he had no stomach for this mode of
travel and he stretched out on the couch and closed his
eyes.

At last they felt a thud as the ball was grounded and
the turbulent movement ceased.

Dilke rang Department 7A. Price answered.

'What do we do now?'

'Lord Raglen should be here within the hour, at around
eighteen hundred hours. I'll let you know when he has
arrived. Take the radio with you when you see him, he
may want to talk to you.'

'I have brought Sergeant Wallis's papers and I'll leave
them in this chamber. I will also leave our notes, will you
please have them typed for when I get back?'

Time passed; the hypnotic humming of the gyroscope
imperceptibly lowered in tone; the three men lay looking
up at the spinning flywheel; Olsen fell asleep.

Price rang at about twenty hundred hours. He sounded
jumpy. 'I'm afraid there is a hold up, Captain Dilke, Lord
Raglen will be late; he has gone on to the House of Lords,
it might be midnight when he gets back.'

Bill Olsen lay with closed eyes; 'What about some
grub?' he called.

'We'll need something to eat and drink,' said Dilke. 'I
didn't know we'd be waiting this long.'

'I'm sorry, Captain, but you'll have to hold out until
after your briefing. Lord Raglen may be back sooner than
I think . . .' Price prevaricated. Olsen turned his head
to Dilke, opened his eyes very wide and mocked him with
a smile.

' . . . you'll have a meal later,' continued Price ,'a big
stock has been laid in for you. I'll let you know as soon
as I hear anything.' The line went dead.

The gyroscope revolved more and more slowly; the flywheel was no longer a smooth blur and they could see the
imperfections of its painted surface as it spun above
them. The whine died away leaving only the sighing of
disturbed air; the centre column turned more and more
slowly until at last the rumbling from the ball-race in the

middle of the floor ceased. The huge, gleaming column came to a stop.

The only sound came from Bill Olsen's grumbling belly.

Price rang to say—rather breathlessly—that Lord Raglen had left the House.

Fifteen minutes later he told them to leave the chamber for their briefing. They walked down the ramp and left the transporter.

The sphere had been placed on the edge of the blotting-pad on Raglen's desk. The three men walked out on to its snow-white surface. It was lit like a Siberian prison camp with the harsh glare from a low-set desk lamp. They paused with their eyes screwed up against the light, then they marched in step with their long shadows to the middle of the pad.

A big, white shape lay on the desk next to the pad. Because of its huge size they did not, at first, recognize it as a hand. It lay palm down on the leather top, white, hairless and quite still. Its soft skin was spotted with irregular brown freckles. Its nails were surgeon clean and polished smooth. The wrist was cuffed in dazzling white and Dilke's eyes travelled up the black sleeve to the pyramid of the body and head. He had adjusted to the scale of plants and manmade things, but the first sight of this colossal body shocked him with a new awareness of his insignificance.

The face was dimly lit from below by reflected light from the white paper. They stared up at the swollen jowls and the shining forehead, freckled where it met the thinning sand-coloured hair. Lord Raglen's right hand held a cigar to his mouth, poised horizontally. A trickle of smoke leaked round its butt where it was moored centrally between the fat, pouting lips, curling into the twin tunnels above. The pouchy, half-closed eyes gazed across the dark room.

Major Price's voice came simultaneously over Dilke's radio phone and the desk intercom.

'Captain Dilke and his men are ready, sir.'

Raglen's cigar end glowed; a billow of smoke issued from the mouth and obscured the face and hand. Out of the cloud the cigar floated away across their heads. The hand carried it into the shadows beyond the desk light and deposited it in a glass ash tray. A slow, peer-of-the-realm voice came down, carried on a gust of cigar and brandy fumes. The great moon face inclined towards them and the last of the smoke floated away like vapour across a mountain top.

'You men are commissioned to do a job which is important to this department. I am told that miniaturization is the thing of the future. I am not convinced of this. It is your job to make a success of this undertaking; the results you get will affect my evaluation of the project and, therefore, the future of the programme. The mission is important not only for itself but also because of its wider significance.'

There was a long silence; Dilke spoke into the radio phone.

'I have not yet been told what we are to do, Lord Raglen.'

The silence continued.

Major Price's voice came over the office intercom.

'Captain Dilke would like to speak to you, sir.'

'What?'

'On his radio telephone, sir. Your ear, sir.'

Lord Raglen's right hand went up to his ear; a plug like a deaf aid protruded from it. He frowned and tapped the plug with his right forefinger and the thud and crackle in Dilke's ear made him grimace.

'Yes?'

'I have not yet been told what the mission is, sir.'

Lord Raglen jerked at the cord of his earpiece, the plug came out.

'Price will tell you all that.'

The freckled hand disappeared then reappeared in the pool of light holding a plastic dome. The transparent dome dropped over them, thudding on to the soft blotting paper; their ears popped under the pressure of the compressed air. They looked up; the roof of the dome was a magnifying lens, thirty millimetres across; in it a huge eye appeared, soft-edged at first but suddenly sharp as it descended. The shutter of the eyelid flashed as the eye adjusted its focus, then it stared fixedly down. The eye of God: tinged with yellow and fretted with blood

Feel the Black Velvet.®

Smooth Canadian.

DON'T CROWD ME!

Fed up with recreation land offers like political campaign promises? Things closing in on you these days? It's nothing five acres of unspoiled New Mexico won't cure. Imagine having more land than 40 city-size lots all your own. Land to camp, hike, hunt, explore historic ruins, build or plan for the future on. And just over the mesa is a well-stocked 25-mile-long lake and a popular, fully developed New Mexico State Park with plenty of fishing, boating, swimming and fun. It's your land, your legacy, your investment in your family's future.

But act now! You won't find much recreational land with all Ranchos Lake Conchas has to offer still available at this price.

Own 5 acres for just $25 a month (total price $2975). No money down. No interest or carrying charge. Money back guarantee. Immediate possession.

Feel the Black Velvet.®

Smooth Canadian.

DON'T CROWD ME!

Fed up with recreation land offers like political campaign promises? Things closing in on you these days? It's nothing five acres of unspoiled New Mexico won't cure. Imagine having more land than 40 city-size lots all your own. Land to camp, hike, hunt, explore historic ruins, build or plan for the future on. And just over the mesa is a well-stocked 25-mile-long lake and a popular, fully developed New Mexico State Park with plenty of fishing, boating, swimming and fun. It's your land, your legacy, your investment in your family's future.

But act now! You won't find much recreational land with all Ranchos Lake Conchas has to offer still available at this price.

Own 5 acres for just $25 a month (total price $2975). No money down. No interest or carrying charge. Money back guarantee. Immediate possession.

vessels. They stared back into the void of the iris for a long minute.

The eyelid shuttered twice, a sheet of liquid flowed across the eyeball and streamed in a line of bubbles along the lower lid. The eye receded into a blur and vanished.

'Show over!' said Olsen.

The magnifying dome tilted and swung away off the blotting-pad leaving them standing in a swirl of cigar ash. Lord Raglen had vanished. They heard the thud of a closing door.

'Major Price, I am still waiting for my briefing.'

'Behind the transporter is a cigarette box with a door in its side. If you go in you can eat and I will give you your brief later. In an hour I will ring through on the Marconi and then we can talk.'

They looked back across the white blotting paper, past the shining sphere, and saw beyond it a dirty yellow cigarette pack. The words TIGARI DE PRIMA were crudely printed in curly brown lettering on the side of the pack. Beneath the horizontal stroke of the T was an open door; through it a light shone.

Inside, it looked like the cabin of a space-ship and smelled like a Turkish cigarette factory. To the left of the door was a wall of cupboards. Facing was a big Marconi transmitter/receiver; it was switched on and threw out a noise like discreetly frying bacon. On the right of the door was a deep, waist-high platform which curved up to the ceiling. There were three recesses moulded into the curve of the platform, lying side by side and cast in the shapes of human bodies with shoulder straps which crossed over and clipped on to broad lap straps. The platform was moulded in white polystyrene, the cupboard doors were black Formica, each one numbered in white. One of them was open: inside were racks of food containers, beneath was a refrigerator holding bottles of beer and lager. The three men assembled a feast on the platform, then lay back in their padded couches and took a leisurely supper. They dozed until Major Price came through on the radio.

Their mission was espionage: they were to be taken overland to Rumania; they would be dropped off near

a military camp and would find their way to the room
of a Marshal Volsk; they would attach radio transmitters
to the head of Volsk and would then return to England.

Dilke's face went pale with anger. 'Scott-Milne and
Olsen are not in Intelligence, Major. They never agreed
to *this*. I will not ask them to go!'

Disregarding signs of consent from his companions
he continued savagely, 'And what has espionage to do
with the population explosion, Major Price? Does Professor Mathis know about this?'

The silence lasted for seconds.

'You *were on loan* from the department, Captain
Dilke.' Price's voice was conciliatory. 'This won't affect
Professor Mathis's programme.'

At last Dilke nodded acknowledgment of the signals
from the volunteers.

'It will if we don't get back,' he grated.

The transporter TIGARI DE PRIMA was stuffed with equipment for the mission. In addition to frozen foods and
survival packs of glucose and chocolate there were maps,
compasses, watches and three small radio transmitters—
each of which was to be attached to Volsk. There was a
wardrobe containing three sets of clothing, custom
tailored to each man's size, ingeniously designed
to take maps, cameras, lenses, with stiff new harnesses
to carry their bows, and with pouches for the miniature
radio transmitters—they were meticulously thought out
to the last zipped-up pocket. The clothing was made
from a smooth wind-proof fabric of an almost fluorescent
yellow colour.

'Major Price. Which bloody maniac had the idea of
dressing us in bright yellow? We'll shine like glow-
worms in these! Has he never heard of camouflage?'

Bill Olsen put in an aside, 'Ask him whose side he's
on.'

Major Price was too tired and too flustered to exert
his seniority and, when Dilke pressed him for more information about the mission, he gave—by the early
hours of morning—more background knowledge than
he had intended. The cigarette box was to be taken by
two agents posing as a man and his wife on a car tour

of Europe. They would travel by boat to Ostend, drive through Belgium, Germany, Czechoslovakia, Hungary, and into Rumania. There they would drive along the road from Arad to Bucharest. Volsk was Commandant of the Rumanian Tank Exercise and Gunnery Ranges on the plains north of the Transylvanian Alps. The box would be dropped off at the roadside near the camp buildings. They must then find their way to Volsk's bedroom and attach the transmitters to his scalp. When the mission was complete they would return to the box and radio the British Office in Bucharest and the tourists would pick them up on their return trip. The map pockets in each jacket contained identical sets of papers: a large-scale map showing the camp and the country which surrounded it, an aerial photograph showing the camp buildings within the perimeter of the army ranges, and a photograph of Marshal Volsk.

Dilke had a lot of questions.

When and where were they starting? In time to catch the Friday night car-ferry from Dover.

How long would the journey last? About four days: they should be in Rumania on Tuesday.

How would they be dropped? The agents would decide this.

How were they to attach the transmitters to Volsk's head? There were loops and clips which would enable the transmitters to be attached to hairs on the scalp.

Yes, but how were they to get on to Volsk's head? They must use their initiative.

Why three transmitters? It increased the chances of success and decreased the risk of all the transmitters being dislodged later.

What was all the camera and binoculars and radio paraphernalia for? The backroom boys would like a field test of the equipment, Dilke would have to report on it on his return.

And the space-fiction seats? It would be a rough ride.

'The whole bloody thing sounds like a rough ride,' growled Dilke. 'What's it all for? Why is it important to bug this Marshal Volsk?'

'I don't think I should go into that, Captain Dilke,' Price said wearily. But he grudgingly explained: for some

years top military men of Communist central Europe—
Hungary, Bulgaria, Rumania—and Russia—had held
secret annual meetings; M.I.5 had had little interest in
these meetings till this year when they learnt that General
Fok Sing was to attend. General Fok Sing was in command on the border between China and India; M.I.5
were interested in the reason for his being at a meeting
which had, till now, been routine and localized.

'You mean they're setting up an invasion?'

'I don't mean that at all, Captain Dilke, we are merely
interested in the meeting.'

Because he was to be this year's chairman, Volsk
would be present when any important matters were discussed: the transmitters would beam every word spoken
by him and to him directly back to London.

They heard a closed-mouth yawn. 'I am sure everything will go well, Captain Dilke. If you need more information you can speak to me here, if you radio from
Europe please set it on "scramble". You and your men
have my best wishes, and I'm sure I speak for the
whole department.'

'Major Price.'

'Yes, Captain Dilke?'

'I've been deceived.' Dilke's voice was bitter but
resigned.

There was a long hiss of silence.

Olsen grinned. 'Good night. The poor bastard must
be properly done in.'

2

They fastened their harnesses when the container was picked up, dozed during the Channel crossing and woke when the car roared up the incline from the car-ferry into Ostend.

'Sounds like a Volkswagen,' said Henry. 'I once had a Volkswagen . . .' They looked at him expectantly. 'I called it Otto,' he smiled.

They spent three days eating, drinking well and listening through the half-opened door to the conversation of the two agents. They were a business-like pair, driving in shifts and with little to say about the scenery. As they passed over each border the man put his mouth near the box and stage-whispered the information to them—he had taken to smoking Gauloises and he sounded as though he thought he sounded foolish.

At the dawning of the fourth day they halted—then started again—then he breathed 'Rumania' on them. They shut the door, kitted up, lay in their couches and waited. The road was rough and they strapped themselves in. Dilke watched the clock. It was eight-thirty when the chattering engine slowed and the car came to a stop. They heard the click of an opening door, felt suddenly airborne, had a sensation of falling and then the box hit the road with a crash. They lay hanging in the straps at a steep angle, unclipped the harnesses, slid off the platform and went to the door. Above the idling of the engine they heard a shout.

'Bucuresti?'

'Înaintează! Înaintează!' a harsh voice replied.

Dilke slid open the door; the car revved and a cloud of dust and exhaust fumes flew in. Dilke looked out; the 'Move on!' man with the gravel voice was on the other side of the ploughed road looking like a refugee from the Don Cossack Choir. He had an automatic rifle over one shoulder and was squinting down the road at the receding Volkswagen. A black Alsatian on the inside of the high perimeter fence barked a surly good-bye at the back end of the car until it was out of sight, then it flopped down in the sun and rolled out a yard of wet tongue. Baggy-pants spat copiously into the road and strolled across the front of the main gates.

After the resonance of the small chamber the silence of the open sky and flat Rumanian plains felt tangible. From far away came the sweet, meandering song of a skylark.

Dilke's squad started the long hike across the road.

It had been churned up by ox carts and tank traffic till it was like a miniature battlefield. They crossed rough valleys littered with the spilled maize trash from carts, avoided the stagnant lakes of diesel oil and hills of dung till eventually they came to the roadside. Here the grass was cropped short but inside the fence it grew rampant. An insect track brought them to the heavy wire fence, woven into a diamond mesh. The metal was rough, giving hand- and foot-holds, and they scrambled up a steeply angled strand till they saw, above the swaying grass stalks, a high grey shed.

Dilke got out the aerial photograph to plot a route. In the picture there were two arc lights hanging over the camp gates but when they looked along the fence they could see no electric cable.

He pocketed the photograph. 'Let's find that cable.'

It was twined down the gatepost and snaked off through the grass like a smooth Macadam highway. They climbed on to it and in two hours were in the shadow of the building. Beside the huge metal-framed shed stood a small brick outhouse. The cable went into it and from inside came the 'buff, buff, buff, buff' of a generating engine.

It was mid-morning. Two giant mechanics in army

dungarees sat in the sun with their backs to the shed wall: one with his eyes closed and a burnt-out cigarette between his lips; the other, with a tin mug on the ground beside him, turned the pages of a letter.

The micro-men watched. The reader read his letter slowly three times then raised the mug to his lips. He spat out a mouthful of tea and shot the rest of the liquid into the road with a grunt. The sleeper awoke, relit the yellow stub and they stood up and sauntered into the shed.

Dilke and his companions slid off the black cable on to the shed's concrete surround. They walked across the path on which the mechanics had rested and came to the entrance into which they had vanished.

It was a vehicle repair shop. Beyond the sunlight which streamed into its wide entrance the gloom of the interior was lit by a single bulb and a streak of light from a distant doorway.

The aerial photograph had shown more buildings beyond the shed. The shortest way to them was diagonally across the shed to the door. Its floor was equal to the combined areas of Dilke's garden and the allotment, it would be like a ten-mile journey. Inside the shed several Bistrita tanks were backed up against the wall on the right. Within the entrance was an inspection pit with a staff car parked over it. Beyond the pit was the servicing area: a battery-charging unit and a long metal bench that disappeared into the shadowy interior.

'Let's go!' Dilke gave it an American inflection. As they approached the staff car the great head of a mechanic appeared above the edge of the pit. He squinted up into the chassis of the car—a brown cigarette stub nipped between his lips—pushed a grease gun against a nipple, then pumped the gun. Black grease oozed out of the bearing and fell in a thick dollop on to his brow. He expelled the cigarette with a Rumanian obscenity, took the grease on his thumb and transferred it to the edge of the pit where it sat like an enormous black slug. When they reached the end of the pit Dilke looked back; the greaser had finished; he squatted at the bottom of the great canyon, a monster illuminated from below by his inspection lamp.

They travelled north-west with the battery chargers on their left, and the vast shadowy plain before them. The smells of the countryside were replaced by the smells of petrol, oil and grease, of burnt metal and caustic acid. On a bench high above them a row of vehicle batteries were on charge, with huge dials registering their amperage. Straw-wrapped glass containers of acid and discarded battery cases stood beneath the bench. The plain was littered with boulders with gleaming green-and-white facets.

'Keep away!' Dilke warned when Henry walked closer to examine one. 'It's ammonium chloride.'

A crack in the concrete floor started under the battery bench and went as far as they could see to the north. The wide ditch was filled with acid and a vapour rose from it which stung their eyes and nostrils.

They retreated and looked for another route. High overhead a twelve-foot steel girder, supported on foot-high ammunition boxes, bridged the ditch. The lid of the nearest box lay open and they climbed its inclined plane on to the girder which stretched, a smooth cause-way, into the distance. With the high steel wall of the L-section girder on their left and the shed floor stretched out below them they set off.

They crossed above the reeking ditch. From the bridge they could see it winding over the concrete plain; acid had crystallized along its edges and, in the distance, had spread in a brittle film across the floor.

They were jubilant.

They walked quickly along the wide girder and had almost reached the middle when they heard the sound of footsteps and the scrape of metal on metal.

They stopped. Three hundred millimetres ahead a huge hand came over the wall and gripped the girder. It was dirt ingrained and nicotine stained, with bitten-down nails and grazed knuckles.

The girder swayed beneath them. A black metal helmet with an acre of smoked glass in its front loomed over them. An acetylene cutter appeared with a needle-point of blue hissing from its nozzle. The hissing point roared into a billowing yellow flame then diminished to a slim blue-green tail.

The cutter took a tentative bite at the edge of the girder then moved steadily across the roadway before them. A fountain of sparks went up into the roof and showered down like meteorites. The glare and the roar blinded and deafened them; the stench from the burning steel choked them. They crouched in the angle of the girder to shelter from the hurtling white-hot boulders. The metal was incandescent where the torch cut into it, fading to straw yellow, dull red and purple. The dull colours advanced down the road towards them. Olsen gave a yell and they turned and ran through the hail of boulders. There was an echoing clang of metal falling on concrete, the windy roar stopped, the torch-flame blipped, the only remaining sound was the singing of cooling steel. They ran till they reached cold metal then stopped and looked back.

Their bridge was gone.

They stared at its glowing end. 'That's buggered that!' panted Olsen.

He pulled off his boots and examined their smoking soles. 'Jesus, Mat,' he said fervently, 'I thought we'd bought it!' He stood up, danced his toes on the cold steel, then slung the boots around his neck.

'Let's move before he comes back for the rest of it,' said Dilke. They stood on what had been the middle of the girder and as they could see no way down they trudged back to their starting point and descended to the floor.

They stood for a minute at the foot of the box, undecided about their next move. A head appeared from the turret of a distant tank, shouted 'Yakov!' then disappeared. Yakov left the bench at which he was working, climbed on to a tank track and looked down into the open turret. A starter motor whirred and coughed then coughed again.

'I think we'd be better taking the back roads,' Bill Olsen waved at the shadows beneath the workbench. 'It might be safer. They've only got to move out a tank when we're in the middle of the floor . . .'

Dilke stared at the tanks, and at the mechanic who had pulled down a block and tackle from a pulley in the roof and was feeding a chain into the tank's interior.

'Yes. All right, Bill, let's do that.'

They turned from the open floor and walked under the battery-charging bench. They passed an old rubber glove and an acid-encrusted funnel. A litter of straw lay on the floor and they crawled under and over its criss-crossed stalks till they came to a clearing. Their view of the mechanic was now obscured but they heard the steady rattle of chain as he hauled something out of the tank.

They crossed the clearing into the shadow of the workbench. A pair of torn dungarees, stiff with grease, rose in a series of folds before them. They climbed till they reached the summit. Overhead, like the roof of a colossal railway terminus, was the underside of the bench, its thick timbers supported on a heavily strutted metal frame. A long perspective of dusty webs hung in great loops and skeins: an aerial graveyard for ten thousand gnats. Beneath the webs lay a black country, a floor littered with lost and discarded objects, all coated with a film of grease to which dust and strands of cotton waste adhered.

They descended the slopes of denim and made a way through piles of debris: gigantic spark plugs, rusting pliers and broken hacksaw blades.

Progress was slow and by late afternoon they had travelled only halfway down the shed.

A shallow lake of sump oil barred their way. They stepped on to its yielding, pitch-like surface and walked warily across it. As Henry leapt from the lake to firm ground his foot broke through the skin and he sank to mid-calf in the viscous fluid. They scraped off most of it, then Bill Olsen cut a strand from a mountain of cotton waste and teased out its fibres to make a coarse brush. This removed most of the residue and they sat by the lakeside and rested. Henry wiped his hands on his tunic and distributed slabs of chocolate. While they ate he touched Olsen's arm and pointed to a huge black shape above them; roughly triangular, it reminded Olsen of the giant manta rays he had seen in the Persian Gulf. Suspended amongst the hanging webs it swayed in a rough hammock at the end of a tangle of filaments. It was a moth, swathed in web and embalmed in the ubiquitous coating of grease.

'I'm surprised to see *any* insects in this *stinking* hole,' growled Olsen.

'You'd be surprised where insects get, Bill. There is a species of fly which starts life in the crude oil around South Californian oil rigs and which lives nowhere else.'

Dilke had left them to look for a way ahead and he shouted and waved from a hill of iron filings. Rust had welded the filings into a solid red mass and they ran up it and joined him.

Beyond the ridge a big yellow box lay in a hollow. Dilke smiled at their startled faces as they read the words: TIGARI DE PRIMA.

The transporter! It had sunk into a bed of rusty filings and the card was soaked with water. They approached it and Henry touched the mould which spread over its side and smelt the smell of decomposed card. There was no door into it. It was an old pack, discarded months before, a mechanic's oily thumb-print marked its surface.

During the afternoon they heard the men working on the tank engine and the bench creaked when a heavy weight was lowered on to it, disturbing a shower of particles from above.

But now the clink of spanners and the sound of drilling stopped.

Yakov sang in the Italian style, full of heart and excessive vibrato. They heard the sound of giant feet receding then the crash of a closing door and the workshop was silent.

Olsen checked the time. 'Clock-watchers!' he said.

'No Stakhanovites, they,' murmured Henry.

The light had so diminished that they stumbled over the rubbish in their track, so they left the shelter of the bench and travelled in the open. Here the floor was swept clean and the tools left lying at the end of the day were polished bright with use.

The area near the bench was smooth but beyond it heavy tanks had created a desolate landscape of cracked concrete, and the clay droppings from their tracks littered the floor.

Their way to the shed door was across this area of ravines and clay mountains.

This was the most arduous part of their journey; they followed the edges of ravines, scrambled across valleys filled with rubble and made detours around cliffs of dried mud. In the fading daylight it was difficult to keep a sense of direction and they sometimes crossed and recrossed the same area. At last the only light came from the single bulb high in the roof; the night sky was framed in the open end of the shed.

Slowly, within the silent shed, a pervasive sound grew, a murmuring, singing sound, which came from above.

To Dilke and his companions the vast interior was a black universe. They turned up their faces and stared into the darkness, blinking at the fixed yellow star with its whirling constellation of insect satellites.

The volume of sound fluctuated, its timbre became harsher, a groaning note insinuated itself and grew louder. There was a sharp report—then silence.

The three men stared at each other.

From another direction the sound began again and built up to its climax. But now it was overlaid by a counterpoint of other noises until it seemed to come from everywhere, from nowhere, from within their heads, from outer space.

The great shell of the building was cooling in the night air. Its skin of sheet metal bolted to steel contracted minutely. The cosmic groans of stresses building up and of tensions suddenly released continued as the men walked on in the dim light. The noise faded as the structure adjusted to the night's temperature. A last sharp crack echoed down the shed, then there was only the sound of their footsteps and the tapping of moths hitting the high lamp.

A huge clod lay in front of them, moulded into a block by the tank track from which it had fallen. They climbed it to get a better view of the way, and from the top they saw before them the dark line of a hose-pipe leading to a tap by the door. They descended, hurried across a rough plain and got on to the pipe with difficulty. Olsen scrambled up from Dilke's shoulders, then he pulled up Henry and they both dragged up Dilke. The hose-pipe was grooved along its length and they walked in file in the top groove. Dilke's eyes wearily followed the undulating path which swept in big curves to right and left. Henry walked like an automaton, Olsen in stolid silence.

At last the pipe rose in a steep curve before them. Water leaked from the tap and ran down the groove in which they walked; they drank from the stream then jumped to the floor. The pipe had brought them to within a few hundred millimetres of the great door. A strip of cloth which had been used to bandage the leaking tap had fallen to the ground.

They had not slept for almost eighteen hours and they crawled into a fold of the cloth and lay down.

The silence in the shed was almost complete. Only the moths orbiting the bulb moved. The men dozed, disturbed occasionally by stunned moths crashing comet-like to the floor—but finally they were lulled to sleep by the soft flutter of wings.

They slept till the morning breeze rattled the door.

'Let's go, fellers.' Bill Olsen mimicked Dilke's simulated Americanese.

They sluiced cold water on to their faces, then walked beneath the door. It swung above them, crashing violently and intermittently against its catch.

It was dark and cold but they were glad to be out of the workshop. A flush of light marked the skyline. They sat at the top of a cement slope which led to a footpath and watched the light creep up from the horizon. The swaying grasses, at first silhouetted against the sky, gradually turned green. A lark trilled as if half asleep. The bird's song and the smell of grass and damp earth were sweet after the journey through the dirt and stink of the shed. Henry lay back while his companions searched the photograph for a track to the main camp building.

The army had taken over a farm. Its roughly plastered, whitewashed walls were turning from grey to pink in the changing light. A long, rambling, single-storey building, it was partly obscured by the rampant vegetation of a derelict kitchen garden.

Dilke and Olsen stood up.

'You O.K., Henry? I'd like to push on.'

'He's a growing lad; needs his sleep!' laughed Bill Olsen, and lightly kicked the sole of Henry's outstretched foot.

They walked down towards the footpath and Henry opened his eyes, sat up smartly, and with sudden energy pursued them.

A forest of grass bodering the path concealed a gutter—just a shallow depression running parallel with the pathway leading to the house. They had seen it on the photograph and when they came to where the grass was sparse they turned off the grit-strewn track and walked through the forest of brittle stalks to the gutter, which was filled with fine sand.

At seven, two giant figures passed. Their heavy footfalls on the gravel and the swish of their stiff overalls signalled their approach; their dark shapes loomed for a moment through the screen of grass and then diminished rapidly towards the shed.

The flat, sandy bed of the gutter stretched before them. In places the grasses leaned from each side and meshed together overhead. Bill Olsen was reminded of the Zambesi—in the morning sun the white sand gleamed like water.

At eight they walked into a tunnel of overhanging foliage. They heard a dry, rustling sound overhead, a clutch of newly hatched grasshoppers hung inverted from stalks of grass.

Henry shot at a hopper but only injured it. It crashed down, falling from blade to blade, dislodging one of its fellows in passing. The dislodged insect fell on its back a little distance from the men, frantically kicked itself upright and went off in short hops. They watched it go out of the shadow of the over-hung foliage and up the dry bed of the gutter till it disappeared round a bend.

The injured hopper hung by one leg from the lowest grass stalk. It hung for a minute, aimlessly moving its other legs and its antennae, then it fell at their feet. Black-eyed and pale-bodied, it was somehow pathetic in its helplessness. They despatched, dismembered and grilled it, the flesh within the as yet unhardened casing was white and succulent; Bill Olsen produced three cans of beer to accompany the meal.

By nine o'clock they had moved on.

The wide, sandy road over which they had travelled at last faded out; they scrambled through undergrowth and came out on to a cement path beside the building. A brush-width of paint had been run along the base of the whitewashed wall, its brilliance was hard on their eyes, but its broad, smooth surface made a good path and in a short time they came to the end of the wall and turned the corner.

The building was in the shape of an L: the long leg of the building was on their left; facing them, and at right-angles to the main building was an extension. A rough stone table stood outside, shaded by a vine which grew over an openwork awning. A man sat at the table on a tubular chair.

The sun blazed on the forecourt which lay between them and the distant figure.

As they set off across the coarse grey surface, sunlight flashed from the broken flints and split pebbles embedded in the concrete surface. Within an hour they reached the shelter of a bank of nettles and from its shade they watched the man. He sat with his forearms resting on the table top, with his peaked military cap on the table at his elbow. He was of medium height, very broad, his neck was short, his head round, his hair close cropped.

'Bratislav Volsk. Born 1913. Eldest child of a family of ten. Son of peasant farmer. Served in Soviet Army during the Second World War. Present rank: Marshal of the Rumanian Army; Tank Training Section . . .'

Dilke remembered the potted biography on the back of Volsk's photograph—he also remembered the picture of the hard mouth and the round peasant cheeks squeezing up the small black eyes—this was unmistakably Volsk.

He sat under the vines, his hands flat on the table, a thin cigar like a factory chimney smoking between two fingers. He was immobile, gazing at the plains which shone in the mid-morning sun. From the doorway at his back came the muted sounds of an office: typing, telephones ringing, file drawers being slammed. He sat without movement for fifteen minutes. An orderly came out with a pile of papers and stood beside the table; only Volsk's eyes moved; they swivelled sideways at the man, then his right hand reached out and took the papers. The man saluted and re-entered the building. Volsk placed the papers before him, scratched a match along the table top and relit his cigar; he picked up a pen and began signing.

His movements had been deliberate and slow but now he signed the letters fast, turning the sheets like a sorting machine. He pushed them aside, anchored them against the slight breeze with his cap and returned to his meditation. The orderly came to retrieve the papers and deliver a message. Volsk looked down at his watch, nodded, extracted a pack of Cuban cigars from his breast pocket and lit one; smoked it, glanced again at his watch and walked stiffly indoors.

'That's our man,' said Dilke. 'He may come out after lunch; let's get a bit nearer.'

They walked under the table and began to climb the trunk of the vine. But before they reached the table top Volsk had returned, he was seated again when they climbed on to it. A strand of the vine lay across one end of the table and they sat beneath its leaves to recover their breath and eat some of their rations. The table top was a slab of marble; squashed and dried-out cigar ends lay under the leaves and the yellow burnmarks of abandoned cigars marred the blue-veined top. A smell of body odour and garlic drifted down the wind.

Volsk had a busy afternoon: he dictated some letters; went indoors to take telephone calls; gave orders to his men. A squad of tanks clattered off the road and parked in the compound which Volsk overlooked; the tank corps commandant came to Volsk for instructions, his goggles pushed up on his dust-streaked forehead. A dispatch rider roared up to the side of the building, delivered a message and waited at attention; Volsk sent him off without a reply.

In the later afternoon he was visited by two officers, and his manner, which had been taciturn and abrupt, changed. He switched on a smile, pushed back his chair and stood to shake their hands vigorously. He called for more chairs. Volsk was by turns silently attentive and voluble, slapping the marble top with the flat of his hand to emphasize his points. His batman brought out lemon tea and finally he walked them back to their staff car and said goodbye. Though their arbour of vines gave some shelter from the sun it was a hot day and Volsk sweated heavily. Since they had first seen him, bare-headed and with the top button of his jacket undone, his standard of dress had deteriorated. He now sat with cigars sticking out of one pocket, a khaki handkerchief out of another and his jacket completely unbuttoned. The orderly came to him after the officers had gone, Volsk dismissed him and soon the office noises ceased; his batman left a tray with coffee and a bottle of vodka; Volsk removed his crumpled jacket and threw it on the table; he drew towards him a metal box which had been left by his visitors, unlocked it and took out a manilla folder of papers. He was into overtime: poured a generous vodka, lit up a new cigar and started work. He skimmed rapidly through the papers, then with pen in hand began again and read more slowly, adding notes in the margins.

Henry had used his camera during the day to photograph the camp surroundings . . . Volsk . . . his visitors . . .

Dilke decided to take some pictures himself. He climbed higher up the vine so that he could look down on the table. It took him an hour to reach a point which was sufficiently high and clear of foliage to give him a good view. Through the viewfinder Dilke saw the whole of the table and the man seated at it. He sat with his tunic shirt undone, a grey fuzz of hair showing on his chest; his short neck thrust from the open shirt; the ring on his left hand glittered as he turned the pages.

Dilke changed to a telescopic lens; it gave him a close-up of the papers, the hands, the box. The box was old and worn, the steel shining through the chipped blue paint; two combination padlocks lay on the table beside it; a sheet of notes was pasted inside the lid; the box contained more folders.

Dilke photographed each paper as Volsk turned it up; the light was failing but he went on exposing a second film even after his meter had stopped registering the light: the backroom boys might squeeze an image out . . .

Volsk locked away the papers and Dilke rejoined Henry and Olsen and they sat under the leaves amongst the stale tobacco shreds and waited.

Volsk drank steadily till it was quite dark under the arbour, the intermittent glow of his cigar lighting his profile.

They heard a squeak and a thump as he recorked the vodka, saw the flying red parabola of his cigar butt go up through the vine leaves and out into the wasteland. His chair scraped on the rough concrete and he walked from under the arbour and urinated into the black tangle of nettles, gazing at the moon which rose over the northern plains. He went indoors; they heard the door slam, a key turn and a light appeared in a window of the extension building behind them. The light illuminated the table; the half-empty bottle of spirits remained; the jacket and the steel box had gone. The window creaked open and was put on its catch. Dilke looked at his watch, it was eleven o'clock, the light went out: Volsk had gone to bed.

3

They had two alternatives: to climb up the vine to the window of the bedroom or climb down and make the long trek into the main building and round to the bedroom. They had no ropes and they realized that they might waste hours climbing to the window and then find that they could not get down to the floor. There were six or seven hours before dawn and Dilke decided that this should be enough time to go the long way round and get into position.

In three hours they were inside the bedroom.

A strip of moonlight lay on the white wall. To their eyes, made sensitive by hours of travelling in the night,

the bedroom and its contents were clear. It was a large
whitewashed room with a bare, plank floor. It contained
only three items of furniture: a camp bed; a monumental
wardrobe with flamboyant peasant decorations on it; and
a huge safe, silvery gray in the moonlight, its metal handle
in the form of a clenched fist holding a bar; the door was
decorated with cast-iron curlicues, surmounted by an
eagle, manufactured—Dilke smiled—in Baltimore.

Volsk's clothes lay in a heap on the floor. They could
see the hump of his bare shoulder above the single
blanket under which he slept. He was as motionless in his
sleep as he had been awake. His deep, slow breathing
filled the room. The bed towered above them, its tubular
legs fitted into sockets beneath the canvas base and they
could see no way up and no way through to the surface of
the bed. They walked beneath it for an hour searching
unsuccessfully for a route. There were only two hours left
before daylight.

They felt defeated.

Suddenly there was a long, heavy sigh from the sleeping
man, then a creak, and he turned in his sleep. The canvas
sagged and stretched and billowed overhead; the bed
groaned; a tumbling avalanche of blanket fell to the floor.
They ran round to the side of the bed. The blanket sloped
up in deep folds like the foothills of a mountain range.

Dilke looked at his companions. Henry's head was
thrown back, his eyes fixed on the receding curves of
Volsk's body. His face had a hard look which had been
absent when he joined Dilke three months before; there
were marks of strain around his mouth and eyes, his brows
were set in a frown. Olsen whistled tunelessly between his
teeth as he secured the radio transmitter at his hip and
tightened the crossbow harness on his back.

'If you're ready we'll start. I'll go first. Follow at intervals of a hundred millimetres. Place the transmitters wide
apart and well down to the roots of the hair or we'll lose
them at his first haircut. I'll put mine near the ear. Put
yours on the crown of the head, Henry. And put yours
somewhere between, Bill . . .' Dilke suppressed an impulse
to shake hands . . . it would be too melodramatic.

'If we get separated we'll meet at the entrance of this
room; if not there, then back at the box.'

Bill Olsen zipped his last zip and made fast his last buckle; he grinned and reached out a hard hand; Dilke shook it and then shook Henry's. He turned and walked into the shadows of the nearest valley which led upwards. When he had ascended to the edge of the plateau he looked back, the climbers below were invisible in the shadows.

The blanket was stiff and rough-textured, decorated with stripes and squares of colour which in the moonlight appeared as a patchwork of greys and blacks. It was like farmland; but beneath him Dilke could hear deep visceral rumbles and soft explosions; a rank smell rose through the coarse weave. He tracked up to the summit of the hill and stood on the edge of the blanket. Two figures toiled up the slope behind him.

Before him Volsk's flesh gleamed in the soft moonlight which was reflected from the wall. Dilke removed his boots and socks and stepped down on the skin; it had a firm, moist feeling, like the body of a whale.

Volsk slept on his right side. Dilke walked up the curve of his chest; the huge thorax rose and fell rhythmically and as he moved higher the deep subterranean thud of the heart became louder. Dilke climbed on the ridge of the pectorals and passed a thicket of hair surrounding Volsk's left nipple—like a cairn on a mountainside in a tangle of rusting wire; he walked along the curve of the deltoid muscle, over the prominent clavicle and into the hollow above the bone. Here, at the base of the neck, the skin was darkened by the sun. The beating of the heart was muted by distance but along the broad column of the neck the carotid artery pulsed to its rhythm. He kept a little to one side of the artery and walked up the thick strap of sterno-mastoid muscle. Dilke stood on the curve of the neck; above and to his left stood the convoluted ear, like something by Henry Moore; on his right were the shallow craters of old carbuncle scars; before him were the first sparse hairs of the head.

The cropped hair rose to waist height, it grew unevenly, its bare grey patches littered with dandruff.

Dawn was approaching: a little colour crept into the black and-white moonlit world. Traces of yellow were discernible in the jackets of the climbers below him; and

behind them the chequered slopes of the blanket were
turning to shades of green and brown—but the effect of
fields and copses was superficial: this huge, rumbling,
throbbing, pulsing hulk was alive.

From the head came a harsh grumbling sound; beyond
the Henry Moore Dilke could see the side of Volsk's
face covered with a dark stubble of unshaven beard. The
jaw muscles were heaving and bunching beneath the skin;
the sleeper was grinding his teeth. The noise lit a spark
of fear in Dilke's mind; it fed on childhood memories of
ogres. The air stank with the fumes of vodka and garlic
and wet cigar butts: it was like approaching the den of
some foul-mouthed beast; a minotaur or a cyclops . . .
for the first time, Dilke felt unmanned.

Olsen was now only thirty paces away, trudging up towards him with his crossbow unslung. Dilke unclipped his
own bow and walked into the hair. The skin had a series
of parallel scratchmarks on it, he walked across the
swollen ridges and around the curve of the ear—looking
for a good site for the radio.

The hairs varied in thickness and in shades of grey. He
chose one as thick as a sapling and, putting down his bow,
he scraped away greasy fragments which clung to the
base of the hair and choked the crater from which it
grew.

He unpacked the transmitter. It was a little bigger than
his fist and was clipped to a metal loop to which a tensioning lever was attached, the lever which would contract the
strap and pull it tight into the rough, scaly trunk of the
hair. He lowered the loop over the hair until the transmitter lay on the skin of the shallow crater then reached
for the lever to tighten the fitting.

From the side of his eye he saw a movement on the
slope above. Bill Olsen was halfway up the curve of the
head, walking with his eyes down, Henry was beyond him
on the horizon. Then Dilke saw the lice. They were
grouped on the head like browsing cattle. Dilke could
clearly see the sucker of the nearest one thrust into the
scalp, the light from over the horizon shone through their
transparent bodies—he could see the blood pulsing into
the stomachs of the creatures.

Olsen, searching for a site for his transmitter, suddenly

came upon a louse, it plucked out its sucker and scurried away, alarming the rest of the small herd. They rushed off leaving tracks in the hair. The scalp moved beneath Dilke's feet; the hair around him stirred—though the air was quite still. Volsk's body shifted uneasily and the muscles of his vast arm moved.

Then a huge, dark shape appeared over the curve of the head.

Volsk's hand.

There was a flash of yellow from his signet-ring, then the hooked fingers sped towards them over the bristling surface of the scalp.

Dilke froze.

Henry flung up both arms, his palms towards the juggernaut, then he disappeared beneath it without a sound. In one smooth reflex action, Olsen dropped on one knee and fired two bolts. They vanished into the whorls on the ball of the nearest finger. A noise like a thousand bulls bellowing hit Dilke and the hand vanished.

The head beneath him jerked convulsively, pressing hard against his feet. He took off into the air; saw Olsen suspended before him like a man on a trampoline; he felt himself somersaulting in the same way, then fell in a spinning curve towards the slopes of the blanket. A kaleidoscope of reds, yellows, browns and greens flashed before his eyes. He hit the slope of the blanket twice and shot over the edge of the bed. The blanket fell from the bed to the floor in a long curve and Dilke whirled down it like a falling ski-jumper. He rolled off the blanket, skidded across the plank floor and fell into the gap between two floorboards. He finished his fall in a cloud of dust, striking his head against the side of the trench.

For a moment he lay on his back, stunned. When he opened his eyes he saw the mountainous naked figure of Marshal Volsk looming over him. Volsk was sitting on the camp bed stamping his feet on the floor; alternately sucking his finger, shaking his hand and clutching it to his belly. 'Isus si Maria! Isus si Maria! Isus si Maria!' Dilke crawled down the long slit trench towards the wall. Volsk rocked backwards and forwards on the bed, suddenly he jumped to his feet and stamped out of the room. By the time Dilke reached the wall a rectangle of pink light from the rising sun had moved halfway down its whitewashed surface.

Dilke's head hurt, his trousers were torn, his knees were skinned and there was a sharp, tearing pain in the fibres of his left shoulder muscle.

4

Dilke sat at the end of the trench with his back against the wall, nursing his shoulder, his eyes shut, his head resting against the side of the trench. His mind remorselessly ran visions of the night's events through the film gate of his memory. Over and over again, as if on a loop of film, he saw the lice; he saw Henry Scott-Miline's death like an old silent movie; he saw Olsen turning a slow-motion somersault, and he experienced again his kaleidoscopic fall down the blanket. His head spun at the memory of it, but worst of all was the flat sense of failure, the bitterness was like bile in his throat. During the early morning Marshal Volsk returned to the bedroom with his hand in a white slab of bandages, carrying with him a smell of antiseptics; he dressed one handed and left.

During that day and the following night Dilke lay up recovering from his fall. The orderly removed the bed and Volsk did not return.

At the dawn of the second day Dilke ate chocolate from his ration pack and started his journey out of the room. He travelled along the edge of the room, into the shadow of the wardrobe, leaping across each trench between the planks as he came to them. He reached the doorway and walked towards the big office.

Then he heard a sound which made his scalp crawl; a deep, chakkering, snarling sound; not an insect sound:— a dog sound. He turned his head and looked back into the shadow of the doorway. From it emerged a huge, black wolf-like creature which reached as high as Dilke's waist. It moved towards him at a half-crouch, advancing each paw slowly.

Dilke's thoughts were completely disorganized, he could not place this insect-sized dog in the scheme of things. For a moment his eyes were fixed on the creature's yellow canines and then he saw around its neck a heavy collar, the chain from it looped and twisted up to stop it trailing on the ground. There was a movement in the shadows and a micro-man stepped out and stood beside the dog. He was a very big man, a head taller than Dilke himself. Dilke's first impression was of the man's physical power and of his handsome smiling face.

He had the physique of a gymnast, with thick slabs of muscle across his chest, round his shoulders and along his arms. He held an olive-green crossbow across his right forearm like a gamekeeper doing his rounds. He had larger-than-life good looks with a wide mouth, straight nose, high Slav cheekbones and blue-green eyes. His naked body was tanned brown from the arched insteps of his feet to the top of his smooth head—and the whole of his face and body was completely hairless.

'Spune-mi, ce faci aici?' he smiled.

'Intelegi Românește?' he smiled again.

Dilke was silent.

The black dog continued its low chakkering snarl. Muscleman slapped it casually across the muzzle with his left hand and it yelped and sat down two paces behind him.

'Do you speak English?' he smiled.

Dilke answered, 'Yes.'

'Ahh!' The hairless skin rose high over the ridge of his brows in a pantomime of friendliness.

'And what are you doing here?'

Dilke could think of no answer.

Man and dog moved near to him. The dog started a low, querulous growl again and the man jerked his head and glared at it.

'Taci!' he spat.

The dog was silent, its ears flattened, its head averted. In the flash of time when he silenced the dog Dilke saw gaps in the man's teeth at the side of his mouth, they gave him an oddly vulpine appearance.

His lips smiled again.

'Turn round, my friend,' he said.

His left hand ran swiftly over Dilke's body; over the jacket pockets, under his arms and between his legs. He patted Dilke lightly on the shoulder, 'I want you to come with me, my friend; I have something which you might like to see.'

He made a gesture which signalled 'Go that way' and a bow from the hips which said 'After you . . .' and they walked into the office and moved along the alleyway between metal filing cabinets and the office wall. For fifteen minutes they walked; Dilke, the man, and the dog.

'What is your name?' the man asked.

'Dilke,' Dilke replied.

'That is a strange name for an Englishman? *My* name is Novi Batzar.'

Dilke turned his head; the man Batzar walked behind and a little to one side, the crossbow still held loosely in the curve of his arm, aimed roughly in the direction of Dilke's right kidney.

'And this is Fulg de Zapada . . .' he inclined his chin to the beast at his side and chuckled deeply, 'it means "Snowflake" '.

'You English keep your hair well.'

Surprised at the irrelevance of the words Dilke glanced quickly at Batzar. 'Zapada; he *also* has kept his hair well—haven't you Zapada?' The dog looked up and gave its tail a flourish. Dilke turned his eyes forward and continued walking, uneasy at the inconsequence of the man's remarks.

They came out of the alley and walked beneath the seat of a chair till they came to a shining metal platform shaped like a scoop. It was thirty millimetres wide, enclosed at the back and sides, and with a waist-high rail across its open front. There were stains of rust in the corners and a big black circle had been painted in the middle of the shining platform. The paint had spread like tarmac and dried with a smooth sheen.

'Please walk on, my friend.'

Dilke ducked under the bar and Batzar did a slow, gymnast's vault over it. Then he did a strange thing: he looked up and walked backwards till he stood in the centre of the circle; he placed his left thumb and fore-finger together and put them between his lips; he blew a long, lazy whistle, the tail of the sound rising sharply at the end.

From the chair above came the sound of creaking leather and squealing metal and a shadow fell across them. The huge hand which cast the shadow came down like a falling block of flats and Dilke went into a reflex crouch on one knee, his hands clutching the rail. The giant stubby fingers raised the platform from the floor and the dog which had remained behind started to leap and bark. The platform remained rocking gently a few millimetres from the ground till two sharp whistles signalled it to rise. The dog's barking touched a peak of hysteria, fading as they left it behind. They soared over the edge of the trestle-table, passing over items of office equipment as big as buildings, a telephone, a skyscraper stack of trays, a typewriter with a sheet of paper rising from its carrier.

On the wide plain below, disposed like huts around a barracks square, were more bits of secretarial gear. A box file, a day calendar in a wooden mount, a carton of spilled paperclips, a typewriter-ribbon tin filled with the crushed fag-ends of Balkan cigarettes.

A ragged blotter, its surface stained with ink blots and the broken flourishes of reversed signatures, was sur-rounded by this clutter and in the middle of the blotter stood a pack of Rumanian cigarettes.

The pack was made of cheap yellow strawboard. A picture was crudely printed in black on its upper surface. It showed a horseman on a galloping horse. The rider sat stiffly erect in the high saddle, fur capped, aggressively moustached, a bandolier across his chest, arms flung out in an expansive gesture.

The horse was frozen in an attitude of mad abandon,

galloping with legs at full stretch, its belly almost touching
the ground.

The drawing had a rough and primitive vitality. PAR-
TIZANUL was printed in sepia in a half circle round the
rider's head and shoulders. The words *Tigari de prima
calitate* appeared beneath the horse's belly.

Dilke looked down on the pack. A knot of apprehension formed in his gut; he flashed a glance at the man
beside him. Batzar regarded him through lazy eyes, his
smile was sardonic; he said nothing.

They made a helicopter landing, the hand depositing
them on the blotter a few paces from the pack; in its side
was an open door.

Batzar's smile had stretched to a grin.

'I congratulate you on your ingenious box of tricks.
You are surprised to see it here? But we have sharp eyes
in Rumania!'

He waved a hand at the now-seated guard who was
lighting a stub of cigarette which he had retrieved from
behind an ear as big as a bowling green. 'Our friend here
found your box of tricks and brought it to us.'

Dilke thought that this gave more credit to the guard's
powers of observation and intelligence than he deserved:
he had probably spotted it while guarding the gate—
trivial things would catch the eye of a bored man—had
picked it up hoping that it contained cigarettes and
showed it round the guardroom as a curiosity before it
was seen by Batzar.

When they entered the container, Dilke found that a
section of the bulkhead had been torn down, revealing an
Ever Ready battery. The inspection panels on the big
radio receiver/transmitter had been removed and its parts
had been dismantled and laid out on the edge of the
platform. The contents of the wall cupboards were also
laid out and Dilke added his camera and maps to the display of wireless parts, binoculars, compasses . . . it looked
like an army surplus store.

Novi Batzar took from the refrigerator two bottles of
beer. Holding them side by side in a big hand he rested
the crown caps on the edge of the ice-box door and

dexterously knocked them off with the flat of his other hand. He made a long arm and offered a fuming bottle to Dilke. He up-ended the other down his gullet, watching Dilke round the side of the bottle; he dropped the bottle to the floor, wiped his mouth with the back of his hand and belched.

'I *like* your English beer,' he said, 'but it has many bubbles.'

Dilke stood watchfully, the bottle held before him, cold between his hands. Batzar did a little jump and perched sideways on the platform. He placed the crossbow within reach, picked up the camera and swung open its hinged back. His right thumb cocked the shutter mechanism and his right forefinger triggered it . . . cocked it . . . triggered it . . . cocked it . . . triggered it . . .

He looked at Dilke through the open back of the camera. Dilke saw the staring eye—magnified by the lens —fixed on him in a series of flashes.

'You make a good camera. Do you prefer a diaphragm shutter? We prefer a focal plane shutter . . . it has some advantages in manufacture. *Every* camera should have a built-in meter; do you not agree? The day of the separate light meter is dead.'

Dilke was noncommittal.

'Is the camera Japanese?'

Dilke said, 'I don't know.'

The brown hands snapped the camera shut and turned it over. 'I can see no serial number, has it *got* a serial number?'

Dilke shrugged.

The hands gently replaced the camera amongst the bargain price equipment.

'We've had trouble with toothache,' Batzar grinned. Dilke decided to take part in the conversation, even though it had once more taken a surrealist turn, 'I'm sorry to hear it. It's a nasty thing toothache—can be very painful.'

Batzar laughed, 'Yes, our first man was killed by his false teeth, his rate of reduction was too fast—he got size-ten teeth in a size-nothing face!' For the first time, Dilke smiled; the idea, though macabre, was funny.

Batzar was encouraged to continue.

'Yes, he was allergic to false teeth . . . and *I* lost some hair.' He passed a palm over his smooth brown head. 'Have *you* had any allergy effects?'

Dilke was silent again.

'False teeth? No hair? Sickness? Deafness? Melancholia? Insanity? Death?' They sounded like words from a patent medicine advertisement.

His interrogator was giving more information than he was receiving but Dilke was tired of the ponderous attempt to trick him into giving information.

'Mr. Batzar, you know who I am and what I am. This game which you are playing will give no results. We are professional agents and you must know that I can not answer your questions.'

Dilke turned and placed the bottle of beer, now warmed by his hands, on the platform. He then faced Batzar.

Batzar still sat easily on the platform, the smile on his face; but it was the sort of smile that has been smiled too long.

He eased himself off the platform edge.

'Very well, Mr. Dilke.' He spoke in a quieter, slower voice with the tiniest emphasis on the 'Mr'. 'We will play another kind of game. You may find it a more entertaining one; at least I think *I* will find it so. Step outside on to the carrier.'

This time the whistled signal was complex, and the guard picked up both the platform and the cigarette box and carried them down the long room, rapidly passing a dozen rough office tables. The end of the room was partitioned off with fluted glass, and behind the partition was another trestle-table; this one was covered with white paper, and on the paper, in front of a rack of test-tubes and some flasks and boxes, stood a microscope.

It was a beautiful but rather antique instrument—big, with a gleaming, lightly oiled brass tube surmounting a turntable which accommodated three alternative lenses. As the transporter approached the top of the tube, Dilke saw a glimpse of a complex arrangement of wheels and levers below him. Then the guard slowly lowered the transporter on to the top of the microscope tower.

They stepped off on to the circular eyepiece.

Dilke walked before Novi Batzar to the centre of the glass floor.

'I have something to show you, my friend.' 'My friend' in Batzar's mouth now had a light, ironic stress which was rather chilling.

He whistled and the hand of the guard moved down below the level of the eyepiece, the tendons in the massive wrist slid under the blue-veined skin as the hidden fingers worked the instrument's mechanism. The glass on which Dilke stood became luminous and he looked down. He was suspended over what appeared to be a huge black-and-white photograph of a face.

It was Bill Olsen.

The head was turned, the face in profile, the brow set in a deep concentrated frown, the sightless eye open very wide. A dark, dried-up rivulet of blood had run out of the bleached hair, down over the temple, and had formed a flaking pool in the curl of the ear. The blood was rusty-red in colour. It was not a photograph at which Dilke stared: he saw a shade of blue in the lips; the tanned skin, now bloodless, had become grey.

Batzar signalled and the guard turned a knurled wheel at the side of the microscope—slowly the face below Dilke's feet receded. Dilke felt a sensation of vertigo and then one of nausea as more and more of the naked body was revealed. The body was fearfully injured; the exposed ribs gleamed through the lacerated flesh and the right leg was stripped of skin and fractured into a grotesque shape. The wrists were bound together.

'Would you like to see how this was done?' asked Batzar.

Dilke's eyes were locked on the body of his friend.

Batzar whistled; the body receded once more; lying beside the dead man was a centipede. It too was dead, curled in a huge S-band fifteen millimetres long; it was on its back revealing the gleaming yellow segments of its belly. On the head, beneath the cruel mandibles, there was a hole surrounded by a flush of green and there was another in the second segment—characteristic crossbow wounds. The corpses were crudely mounted between glass slides, a smear of blood from the man and globules of yellow matter from the centipede had been crushed on to the glass. The light beneath Dilke's feet suddenly changed, the two bodies became black silhouettes; the rag-doll which had been Olsen and the serpentine shape of his killer lay frozen in an obscene dance of death.

'I have something else to show you.'

Batzar had seated himself on the ebony rim of the eye-piece with the crossbow resting across his thighs.

Dilke's breath came in long, dry heaves with an audible gasp at the end of each inhalation; his body shook with the stress of emotion; nausea, grief and rage struggled for dominance.

'I have something *else* to show you.' The voice was malevolent.

The rigid muscles of Dilke's neck slowly turned his head till his eyes looked into those of his captor; the intensity of his hatred glittered through the slits of his eyelids. Batzar brought up the crossbow rather quickly to cover his captive, then he stood up and gave his whistled signal; from the table the guard raised a wooden crate till it was level with the top of the microscope, then he rested it with a thud on the eyepiece rim, holding it there between thumb and forefinger.

The crate was huge—about forty millimetres wide— crudely made, the front covered with a sheet of perforated zinc. A smell came from the box which reminded Dilke of a ferret's cage, but the stink of insect excrement was more pungent and sickening, and he breathed through his mouth to avoid retching.

The box interior seen through the circular holes was dark; Dilke sensed that something within was watching and listening. Batzar struck the front of the cage with the butt of the crossbow and abruptly a hollow, pulsing roar started inside.

Through the holes in the zinc he could see the shining golden bellies of the centipedes. He could not see how many there were because they raced in a pattern of curves and circles over the inside of the cage front, their tracks meeting, diverging and sometimes crossing; their hundreds of legs twinkling and flashing through the perforations. One of them stopped and fixed its multi-lensed eyes on Dilke, it strained to force its head through the hole, biting at the metal and scrabbling with its claws, shaking the whole cage front with its ferocity.

'You have seen our little menagerie. Let us have *another* talk. We will return to your box.'

The giant hand removed the cage and replaced it with the transporter. They stepped on. Dilke clutched the bar, his eyes fixed on the gleaming microscope column as they sank to the table. He stepped on to the table top like a sleep-walker and walked stiffly towards the cigarette pack which lay two hundred paces away. A rack of test-tubes towered above it; the coloured liquids which they contained sparkled coldly in the sun; little clouds of cotton-wool lodged in the tops of the tubes. Beside the rack lay a nickle-plated hypodermic syringe with a needle like a gun barrel, its shining surface picked up the sunlight, broke it into stars and threw them into Dilke's face.

A sudden sharp, prolonged hiss stopped Dilke.

He looked back. Batzar had his eye to a crack in the wall of a wooden crate similar in size to the centipede cage, but without a mesh front. The gaps in Batzar's teeth showed in a wide grin; he called Dilke back with a vigorous signal of his hand and then jabbed a forefinger at the peep-hole. Placing his eye obediently to the hole Dilke found that he was looking through the back of a cage—the cage front was covered in flyscreen wire, finer than that imprisoning the centipede, its bars showed black against the light which shone in. The sun threw a crisscross of shadows on the cage. Dilke's vision slowly recovered from the effect of the sunlight bounced off the hypodermic needle and became accustomed to the dazzling network pattern in the cage.

Suddenly he saw the figure.

It was silhouetted, motionless, pressed against the cage front. Its arms were raised, its hands gripped the bars. It faced outwards but its head was slightly turned— listening.

Three heavy blows struck with the flat of Batzar's hand

on the side of the cage sent a reverberating roar through its interior. Dilke leapt back, but not before he had seen the figure jerk, drop its arms and start to run. In the side of the cage was a door which was locked with a heavy wooden beam dropped into a metal socket. At a sign from Batzar, Dilke lifted the pivoted beam and they walked into the cage. The prisoner had run to the corner farthest from the door and was standing there, one palm against the wall, the other hand pressed to the base of her throat.

The prisoner was a Negress.

She stood stiff and motionless. She was naked, and the bars threw geometric shadows across her body and on to the wall behind her.

Batzar pointed at the floor before him and the girl hurried forward and stood with her arms stiffly at her sides. They were thin, elegant hands which shook with sudden tremors. She was tall, and her body, like her hands, was thin; her breasts, though small, were full and her buttocks had a characteristic Negro prominence. She had high cheekbones and flared nostrils, her skin was blue-black, her lips and nipples deep purple.

Her eyes were wide and fixed on Batzar's face.

Batzar said, 'What do you think of her? We got her from the university. We are doing some lab-tests on her. It is a new approach to miniaturizing—injections instead of drugs. It is very fast and I am pleased with the results till now. No allergies. You see, she has even kept her hair!' he grinned coarsely. The gesture of his hand took in the hair on her head and the black triangle at her groin. The girl's eyes widened still more, showing a rim of white around the pupil of each eye. 'We may breed to micro-size; it may give us more consistency. But the female reproductive system is a complex one and we want to be sure that there are no bad side-effects . . . and we are not sure about sterility. This black will give us an indication . . . we will have her ovaries out tomorrow.'

The girl's eyes closed, and to stop the sudden spasm of shaking in her hands she locked the fingers together in front of her body.

The lecture was over and they left the cage; Batzar tilted the beam and it swung round and fell with a crash

into its socket. Dilke carried with him the picture he had
glimpsed before the door slammed shut; the girl standing
in the middle of the huge cage, her hands clasped, her
head dropped forward on her breast. They walked towards the cigarette pack and when they had entered
Batzar closed the door and leaned his back against it.

5

'Let me be simple about this,' Batzar said. 'We will now
speak plainly to each other. I want you to answer my
questions about things which you must know.' He tilted
his head sideways, his eyes stared, his brow contracted
and he spoke in an undertone. 'I want you to understand
that it is important to me *personally* that you answer my
questions.'

Batzar's capricious shifts of mood—from extrovert
friendliness to malevolence to quiet earnestness disturbed Dilke. Suddenly, and for the first time, the thought
came to him: is he sane?

Sweat ran down from Dilke's armpits.

'If you do not answer me I will feed you to the centipedes—you would like to be a centipede's dinner?' The
threat was almost jocular—the ghastly levity filled Dilke
with sick foreboding. '*No*. It is not nice, your friend did
not like it. I will not hesitate to do the same things to you.
You must tell me everything.'

His manner became brisk. 'These are the things you
must tell me: why you are here? where is the third man?

where are your miniaturizing drugs made? how long have your people been working on miniaturizing? Have you had much allergy in your subjects? How is your technical equipment made—I want *particularly* to know this thing—you must tell me where it is made and how it is made—particularly the radio.'

Batzar said slowly and distinctly, 'If you do not tell me these things I will have done to you the things that was done to your friend. You will be tied and lowered to the centipedes on a rope. It is a horrible and *very* painful way to die. But there is no big hurry,' he reassured, 'you will stay here till morning. Think about your answers tonight. I have shown you the stick—here is the carrot,' he smiled complacently at his command of the English vernacular. 'I am now going to Marshal Volsk; he is not pleased about his hand but I might persuade him to let you keep your life—if you talk to me.' Pause.

'Remember the centipedes.' Pause.

'I will go now.'

He straightened himself and half turned to the door, his bow still aimed at Dilke's belly.

A slick of cold sweat shone on Dilke's forehead. His shoulders suddenly sagged. His head dropped. He said almost inaudibly: 'If I . . . perhaps I could . . .' he turned towards the platform . . . 'the transmitter is . . .' he searched for words . . . 'inside the transmitter it has . . .'

Batzar became very still—his eyes were very attentative and he leaned forward to catch the stammered words.

'Inside the transmitter . . .' Dilke's hand stretched out for the radio transmitter . . . 'it has . . .' he lifted the compact instrument to show to Batzar. But the hand which held it did not pause in its movement; it travelled on in a tight arc of rapidly increasing velocity. Dilke's whole body stiffened into one solid unit which spun on the toes of his left foot—he curled away from the crossbow like a banderillero avoiding the horns of a bull—the radio exploded high up on the side of the big bald man's head with a sound of splintered glass and crushed metal.

The crossbow bolt thudded into the side of the polystyrene platform and vanished.

Novi Batzar fell as if hit by a humane killer. His legs

splayed out, his eyes shut in a tight grimace, his teeth clenched. Mathew Dilke's left knee smashed up into the face of the falling man, his arms flying out as a counterbalance. 'For *Olsen!*' he snarled.

Dilke's legs shook and he leaned, panting, against the platform till the thudding of his heart quietened. Then he dragged Batzar on to the platform, rolled him into the middle of the three depressions and clipped the lap and shoulder straps across his body. Pulling each arm sideways he attached straps from each of the flanking harnesses to the thick wrists and jerked them tight.

Dilke knelt beside the bound figure, a deep cleft of thought between his brows; he stretched out a hand and placed it on the chest of Novi Batzar—the brown skin on the back of his hand almost matched the skin of the tanned body. He crouched for a time, staring at his hand on the big torso, and then he leapt off the platform to the floor and went methodically through his pockets. In the flap-pockets of his windcheater he found a biro and a pad and the remains of his ration pack; in his hip pocket he found a roll of film—he tucked them all into a map case. He unzipped the yellow 'cheater and dropped it to the floor, loosened the belt of his trousers and stepped out of them, stripped off his vest and pants: his body was only a shade paler than Batzar's.

Putting the map case and the one remaining radio transmitter to one side, he swept the rest of the gear—cameras, lenses, binoculars—off the platform and hammered them into the floor with the butt of the crossbow. He destroyed the big Marconi and climbed up to smash the electric clock.

The chambers of the bow were empty; Batzar had fired the last bolt. He smashed the useless weapon against the corner of the refrigerator. He picked up the transmitter and the map case and stood for a moment amongst the litter of cast-off clothing and shattered machinery. He glanced back from the doorway at the strapped-down figure; its head to one side, its arms flung wide. Its left temple and eye were puffed and swollen, and a split followed the upper ridge of the eye socket like a scarlet eyebrow. Batzar's mouth hung open, strings of saliva hung from his jaw; but for the heaving of his chest and the hoarse intake of breath in his throat he could have been a dead man.

Satan crucified.

Dilke opened the door an eye's width. Heat and boredom had put the guard to sleep. He sat tilted in his chair, the peak of his cap shading his eyes. Dilke ran to the cage, unlocked the door and entered. The girl crouched in a corner.

'Do you speak English?'

The girl nodded.

'Come with me.'

She followed him out of the cage across the open ground and on to the platform of the transporter. He took her arm and led her to the middle of the painted circle. 'Sit here,' he pointed. 'You will not be seen against the black.'

Her face showed no sign of comprehension but she sat down with her knees drawn up, clasping them with her arms. Dilke placed himself between her and the guard. He swallowed twice; took a lungful of air; brought thumb, forefinger and the tip of his tongue together and whistled. The long rising sound brought the obedient hand down; it raised the transporter from the table. Two shrill blasts and it shot vertically into the air, flattened out and headed for the big office. The Rumanian Buffalo Bill on the pack diminished and was left behind as if seen from a fast-moving plane.

In ten seconds they were out of the building and in three more they had landed on the table under the arbour of vines.

It was too easy.

The guard stood back to wait for the arrival of Marshal Volsk, his eyes blinking in the late evening sun which shone through the vine leaves. The Negress had fallen on her side and lay curled up, her heels tucked in and her forehead on her knees. Dilke touched her lightly and she stood up.

They stepped down on to the cool surface of the table.

'Run,' he said. The vine cast shifting shadows and they ran through them to the shelter of leaves which lay across the end of the table; the girl gradually outdistanced him, the pale soles of her feet flashing in the sunlight.

The acrid smell of half-smoked cigars hung under the leaves. They clambered down the vine, ran through the rank jungle of nettles and out on to the plains beyond. Dilke had only one thought: to put distance between themselves and the house.

The ground over which they travelled was the area used as a vehicle park. The surface was churned up and powdered by tank tracks and truck wheels; in parts there were ridges and huge boulders; stretches of it had been flattened and smoothed out by the wind. It was a desert.

Dilke ran till it was almost dark, the girl following closely. He found a cave-like recess at the base of a clod of earth. In it they spent the night, it gave shelter from the wind, but it was bitterly cold and they got little sleep. During his periods of wakefulness Dilke's mind worked wearily at the problem of escaping to England.

The escape drill—return to the cigarette box, make contact with the agents in Bucharest, wait to be picked up—was now impossible. He crouched in the dark trying to think of a way to make a rendezvous with the Volkswagen. When morning came he spread out his maps on the ground. The aerial photograph had a numbered grid marked on it and he searched to find an intersection of two lines which fell on the roadway near the camp; if the radio transmitter was working; if he could send a message to Bucharest via London; if the agents in Bucharest had an identical map—then he might be able to fix a meeting place with them. But he could see no way of pinpointing such a place.

They breakfasted on the last of the survival rations and set out again across the plain; the girl still followed silent and close to the preoccupied man.

The sun blazed on the white desert. The heat was stifling, at midday they came upon a winding creek along the bottom of which flowed a shallow stream. They climbed down the eroded side of the creek and drank; Dilke knelt in the shallows and splashed water on to his sweating body. He heard a distant shout. The Negress was staring past him in the direction from which they had come. He jumped up and looked back. A man stood on the edge of the creek, his head was turned from them, he waved a hand and shouted again. One—two—three other men joined him: powerful, naked and hairless; physically they were almost replicas of Batzar. But their heights varied greatly. For a moment Dilke thought that their differences in size were illusory—a trick of perspective—then he realized that the smallest man was only three millimetres high, the tallest was a giant of nine millimetres.

A fifth man appeared; he held a big black dog on a chain, his left eye was swollen shut, a purple bruise darkened the eye socket and shaded off into the brow and cheek.

It was Batzar.

Dilke and the black girl turned and ran through the water, the spray glittered around them in the sunlight, their pursuers shouted, ran along the edge of the creek and found a pathway down. Beyond the creek a flat plain stretched to the horizon. Dilke and the girl ran—at first swiftly, then more slowly and doggedly. Dilke looked back; the five men were running fast and easily behind them. Batzar led, with the dog pulling eagerly at the leash; they had gained a lot of ground. Dilke's breath laboured, sweat blinded him. There was a dull ache in the small of his back; only fear kept him going. They had reached a part of the plain which was uneven and pock-marked with dusty craters. The balance tipped between Dilke's fear of capture and the torture in his lungs and limbs. He could run no more.

'Run on!' he gasped and he stopped and faced about. He stood panting in the dust on the edge of a crater and prepared for his last fight. The crater lay between him and his pursuers. Batzar and the dog were the first to reach its rim; the man started to follow Dilke round the crater but the dog in its eagerness took the direct route, it jerked at the lead and pulled its master down the slope. The rest of the men followed; they slid in a cloud of dust down the crater side and scrambled up the inclined face towards Dilke. Batzar released the dog so that he could climb more easily; as it came snarling over the edge Dilke kicked it hard in the throat. The beast choked and hurtled back on to the climbing men, they tumbled backwards in a heap with the howling dog on top.

Dilke turned to run again when he heard—among the

angry shouts and curses—a shriek. It was not just a
scream of pain but the scream of a man filled with in-
sane fear. The crater bottom, filled with struggling bodies,
suddenly heaved up in a flurry of sand and rocks. The
men and the dog began to sink down into the pit, turning
and twisting and screaming as if they were descending
into a giant meat grinder. Dilke saw the steady rhythmical
flash of the horns of the ant lion.

There was a sound like that of sticks being broken.

He was stiff with horror.

These men he had hated and feared were transformed
by their agony and terror into creatures for whom he felt
a sick compassion.

The ant lion took minutes to drag them below the
surface. The last face to go was that of Novi Batzar. His
head swung wearily; a bubble appeared at one nostril
and multiplied, growing like a froth of crimson detergent.
He gave a deep, grunting cough and belched blood. He
was silent and dead before the polished globe of his head
disappeared. A forest of arms trailed behind the sinking
bodies until only the hand of the biggest man was left; the
fingers stretched and quivered and then relaxed, the hand
fell forward on the slack wrist and slid out of sight.

PART FOUR

1

Dilke knelt in the sand, overcome by the appalling thing he had seen. He averted his head from the smooth, still crater; the black girl crouched behind him. She had not seen the deaths but she had heard the demented howling of the men and the dog and seen Dilke's paralysed horror. Her eyes were wide with shock and fear; she had retrieved the map case and the transmitter from where Dilke had dropped them and she clutched them to her. Dilke went to her and took the case and the transmitter; she dropped her head, and her body shook uncontrollably—in a little while he gently touched her shoulder and she stood up and waited for him to move. He looked northwards into the desert and then back in the direction they had come. There seemed no future in the north and he instinctively felt that there would be no further pursuit. He ran his tongue over his cracked lips.

'Let's go back to the creek.'

They came again to the stream. Dilke drank and then sat in the shadow of he creek bank with the aerial photograph before him.

In a little while he began to laugh silently. The stress of the events of the last two days and the fear of pursuit had inhibited his thinking—now he saw in his more relaxed state of mind that the solution was simple: the pick-up point was down at the lower left of the photograph. There, where the western and southern perimeter fences joined at right angles, was a corner post set in concrete. He picked up the transmitter; its side was dented and its speaker grille was cracked; he shook it and a shower of sand fell out; he placed it to his ear and heard a faint sound like waves in a seashell. When he depressed the 'action' button he could hear no hiss of static—but imagined that the background noise of the stream would mask it. He gazed at the scene before him and collected his thoughts.

The sun lit up the creek bed, revealing the subtle whites and yellows and brown of its eroded sides. Since the death of their hunters the girl had shown less compulsion to stay close to Dilke; now she bathed in the stream, washing away the white dust from her face and body; the deep-blue sky was reflected in the water. Sky, sand, water, girl: it was singularly beautiful.

He put the transmitter to his mouth, '00.25/1 calling Department 7A.'

He repeated the call a dozen times. The girl looked up at the sound of his voice then rose from the water and waded out of the stream, lifting her feet out of the shallows in high, graceful steps, shaking the water from her hands like a cat with wet paws.

'This is an emergency. The original escape plan will not now work. I want you to arrange a new pick-up point with the agents in Bucharest. Listen carefully: in the aerial photograph of the terrain you will see a fence post at the south-west corner of the camp perimeter. Pick us up there; they will need a container because we are on foot. We will be there in six or seven hours. We will wait.'

Though the transmitter might not be working, or the message might have been intercepted, Dilke had done something positive, and he now had a sense of direction.

The girl had joined him in the shadow. She stood before him resting her weight on one leg, her hands clasped behind her, completely silhouetted except for the glimmer of her eyes which were fixed intently upon him.

He touched the ground with his hand.

'Sit down and rest—then we must move on.'

She stooped obediently and sat in the sand beside him.

'What is your name?'

'Hyacinthe,' she replied.

'My name is Mathew Dilke.'

She smiled shyly at his courteous exchange of names.
'What are you doing in Rumania?' he asked.

'I was a student at Bucuresti University.'

'And what were you studying?' he asked with new interest.

'I was taking Economics and Political Science.'

She spoke precisely, yet softly, with a musical inflection
in her voice. Till now, she had followed him like a mute
Girl Friday; he had thought of her as a primitive—someone to be spoken to in simple words.

Now he explained his plans and traced on the map
their route to the pick-up point. He concealed from her
the possibility that the radio was not transmitting and she
eagerly assumed that they *would* be picked up; this, together with Dilke's friendliness, created in her a mood
almost of gaiety. She was eager to move on and to help
in some way and he gave her the map case to carry.

The creek ran towards the south-west and Dilke decided to travel along the bed of the stream till it met the
western fence. They followed the sun's curve till it glowed
red in the west. As they left the desolate plains and approached vegetation they saw more and more wild life,
sand fleas and hoppers watering at the stream, ants crossing the water on their overland tracks. The girl became
fearful and followed Dilke closely once more. At twilight
they reached the towering mesh fence and turned south.
The moon rose round and bright at their backs and lit
their way; but Dilke walked slowly and watchfully, looking intently into the shadows, aware that he was unarmed.
At intervals during their journey he repeated his broadcast
and at midnight they reached the corner post. It towered
three thousand millimetres above them, shining in the
moonlight, supporting the high, coarse-meshed fences,
one going north, the other to the east. The post was sunk
into concrete which was smoothed into a dome round
its base.

They scrambled up the curve of the dome till they
reached the post and Dilke looked along the road to
Bucharest. It lay clear in the moonlight for miles, curving
southwards to the mountains, empty of traffic. The only
sounds were the wind in the high grass and the creaking
of the huge metal post as it stirred in its concrete socket.

They spent a long night sitting in the lee of the post trying to shelter from the wind, but morning found them stiff with cold and haggard from lack of sleep. A glorious sun rose, lighting the rivulets of condensation on the post and the drops of dew on the mesh. The air became warmer; the valley came to life. A man on a horse rode past at a jog, the horse wiry and slim-legged, the rider wearing Genghis Khan whiskers and a sheepskin coat. He rode with his head turned towards the camp, his eyes fixed on the old farm buildings. A boy drove goats along the road. The day passed slowly.

Dilke made a quick excursion for food, leaving the girl to watch, and returned with seeds and eggs and they sat eating and luxuriating in the heat.

Dilke watched the road and talked to Hyacinthe.

Her name was Hyacinthe Yelwa Kasama. Her home was in Uganda. Her father had been a prosperous merchant who found a place in the new government when his country got its independence. Her country received loans and technical assistance from the Soviets and Hyacinthe came to Bucharest on a student grant. Things did not work out well, the new regime in Uganda did not last long, their politics were turbulent and bloody.

The honeymoon period with the Soviets was soon over; Rumanian/Ugandan relations cooled; Negro students were not popular in Bucharest; some of the men were beaten up.

Hyacinthe sat with her back against the post. Dilke watched her profile from where he lay. Her eyes were sad and her voice was low; she gazed across the fields of maize and sunflowers towards the Transylvanian Alps. The sound of cicadas, the tremulous songs of skylarks and her air of resignation combined to create a pervasive air of melancholy.

'My father and my mother and my sisters and brothers were all killed in the massacres in Kampala.'

She leaned her head back against the post and closed her eyes. He reflected that her mood of sadness made her for the moment oblivious of the new dimension in which she lived and which made her old world inaccessible.

There was a shallow crack in the concrete, starting at

the top where the post entered it. Some thistledown fell and rolled across the side of the dome. Dilke caught it, pushed it into the trench which the crack formed and trampled it down till it made a soft and springy mattress. He roused the girl from her doze and she lay down and slept.

He sat and watched the road. During the long hot afternoon not a single vehicle, neither a car nor a tank nor a cart, passed along it.

The sun turned red and lay in the shallow bowl of the valley; the goat herd wandered home; a grey blanket of cloud crawled over the wall of mountains and rolled down their northern slopes. The air suddenly became cold, the soft breeze dropped and the bird and insect song ceased.

Dilke had stopped broadcasting for fear of interception. He was nagged by the fear that the the transmitter was not working. He placed it to his ear; it still sighed like a seashell. And yet he thought he detected a different sound when the switch was moved to 'ON' from 'OFF'—then realized that it could be the effect of a change of the instrument's internal ascoustics.

As it became darker it grew colder.

A gusty wind shook the fence and the post creaked. The wind came from the mountains carrying a hint of snow and ice. Hyacinthe awoke and he climbed down into the trench and crouched beside her. They heard the thud of hooves and a slurred fragment of song on the road from Bucharest and a horseman passed them in the twilight. The horse travelled at a fast walk, its mane and the man's jacket tossing in the wind. The rider lolled in the saddle, laughing quietly to himself.

The storm of wind increased in violence, shaking the fence. A booming sound started in the metal corner post, fluctuating with the waves of vibration that passed along the fence. Low clouds covered the moon, the darkness was complete but for occasional flashes from the floodlights swinging over the main gate. The post rocked and creaked like the mast of a gigantic sailing ship.

Suddenly Dilke felt the side of the trench move against his back and the mattress beneath him shifted. In a flash of horror he realized that the jerking post was opening up a fissure beneath them and he scrambled out and dragged the girl after him.

Now they felt the full force of the wind as they crouched on the curve of the dome; the singing of the fence and the clatter of dry maize leaves blowing in the fields had a soporific effect on him: his eyes closed, his head dropped on to his knees, he was exhausted after his day-long vigil and despite the cold he began to sleep.

2

'Mathew! Mathew!' He felt a hand on his shoulder. He came slowly out from his sleep. 'Mathew!' He opened his eyes, then screwed them up against two stars of light which flared through the swaying grass blades. A car came up the road from Bucharest. He could hear the chatter of an air-cooled engine. The lights dazzled as they grew bigger and he shaded his eyes against them. The headlights, which were about to pass, suddenly swung in towards the fence, brakes squealed, the engine wheezed into neutral, a car door was flung open and a huge figure ran towards them. For a moment it shaded them from the glare, then there was a thud and the sound of metal scraping on concrete and Dilke saw a hand holding a tin box against the curve of the dome.

'Dilke!' The word smelt of Gauloise. On the side of the box he read SICHEL VALVE TUBES. It was partly open. He took the girl's hand and ran to it; he reached up, caught the edge of the box and pulled himself up astride it, then he pulled the girl after him. They both tumbled into the box and Dilke saw the anxious eyes of the agent staring down on them through his glasses. Dilke could almost hear the man counting the seconds; then they were plucked into the air, they heard his feet thudding through the roadside vegetation, the box crashed down on to the dashboard shelf, the door slammed and the gears jerked through first, second, third. The agent left the box partly open and the dashboard light threw a faint glow into its interior.

The box was half-full of yellow valve tubes.

They were big and flexible, like soft rubber drainpipes, and they rolled about the floor of the box as the car jolted over ruts. Dilke sat against the box wall fending them off with his feet when they rolled towards him.

Enclosed by the bare metal walls the cold was even more biting than it had been out in the wind.

Hyacinthe huddled against him, shuddering. He slackened his jaw to stop his teeth from chattering but still they clicked together.

The car stopped at the border.

Dilke dragged one of the big tubes crosswise in the box and jammed the rest against the end wall. The valve tubes were seven millimetres long and about two millimetres in diameter and—compared to the box—were warm to the touch.

'Hyacinthe!'

She jumped up to help him with the tubes.

'No!' he cried, 'Get inside.'

She crawled in and as the engine started he crawled in beside her.

The soft tension of the tube drew their cold bodies together.

They were across the border and travelling west. All day he had been aware—though he had pushed the thought away—that they might never escape, but might die of hunger and exposure at the side of the Bucharest road.

After a while their shared body-heat within the confined tube warmed them. They lay on their sides, facing each other, the girl's long thin body against Dilke; she shifted slightly and the sharp prominence of her pelvic bones pressed into him.

The warmth and intimacy and the sure knowledge that they had crossed the border eased Dilke's tension.

'You *are* a bony girl!' he said lightly. 'We must fatten you up when we get you home.'

The girl's body shook. The jest was a poor one, he put an arm diffidently around her. 'I'm sorry,' he murmured. Hyacinthe stifled a gasp and suddenly, Dilke realized that she was laughing.

The movement within the box was erratic, but the thick rubber wall cushioned them against the jolts.

The road became smoother, the engine sound steadied into a drone.

'I'd *like* to be fat,' she breathed drowsily.

3

The morning light shining through the translucent yelow rubber was soft and warm. Dilke woke and looked down at the girl; she slept against him with her forearms together, her palms on his chest and her head on his shoulder. Dilke felt cramped but did not want to disturb her. His belly rumbled and suddenly he realized that they had not eaten for twelve hours. He gazed out of the tube into the container. Hyacinthe had thrown the map case into a corner of the box, but Dilke knew that it contained no food, and he calculated that it might be three days before they reached London.

As if prompted by his thoughts he heard the woman say, 'We can't leave them like that, John. We must find a better thing to put them in. And let's stop at the next coffee place for breakfast.'

The car drew off on to a gravelled surface and stopped. John bent his head to the glove box and boomed, 'We're just going for a coffee, we'll try and bring you something back.'

After fifteen minutes the key clicked and the door swung open; Dilke crawled out of the tube and peered over the edge of the box. The man was in regulation English holiday kit: slacks, sports jacket, Paisley neck scarf; he sat behind the wheel, deposited a fresh supply of Gauloises in the glove box and cleared a space next to the tin box.

The woman came into the car backwards carrying a cardboard tumbler in one hand and a bar of chocolate in the other. She carefully lowered herself into the seat, produced a bright-blue plastic spoon and, filling it with coffee, laid it on the shelf beside the box. With a penknife the man scraped at the surface of the chocolate, making a small pile of flakes next to the spoon.

Hyacinthe followed Dilke out of the box.

Steaming black coffee lay in the huge bowl of the spoon; Dilke put an exploratory finger into the liquid. It was scalding hot so they turned to the chocolate; the smaller shavings could be picked up and eaten without trouble, and there were fragments of nut amongst the flakes of bitter dark chocolate.

The agents sat and shared the remainder of the bar. They crouched together, their noses almost touching the edge of the shelf, their gaze fixed on the ant-like creatures.

Hyacinthe watched them with big eyes; she was unused to seeing normal beings at such close range. A forest of hair sprouted in the man's nostrils, his eyes slid in the green depths of his sunglasses. A thick red grease of lipstick shone on the woman's lips and the pores of her skin were filled with chalk-like face powder. Their jaws broke up the chocolate like rock crushers.

Hyacinthe was alarmed at their unwinking stares and she glanced at Dilke for reassurance. He sat cross-legged, a slab of chocolate between his hands, chewing stolidly, returning the stares of the gross giants.

The coffee was cold enough to drink and they drank it from their cupped hands, then they returned to the box carrying lumps of chocolate with them.

Dilke rearranged the valve tubes so that the one in which they slept was supported on the others. It insulated them even more from the cold tin floor and the jolting of the car; it was warm but claustrophobic.

It took two days and a night of hard driving to get to Ostend. While waiting in line for the evening ferry to Dover the relief driver thought of the 'better thing to put them in'. She produced from her handbag a circular compact, removed the powder container and put a soft new powder puff into it. She placed it beside their tin bedchamber and the man, who seemed to have been elected spokesman invited them into their new home.

The powder compact was a huge golden oyster, the floor a soft, pink, circular bed, the interior of the half-open lid an enormous round mirror. The puff was as soft as a thousand blades of wool; they waded to its centre and fell back with arms spread. Dilke repressed a desire to bounce up and down like a small boy on a feather bed. Hyacinthe sat up and examined herself in the mirror; she took back her long, unruly hair and knotted it behind her head. Dilke closed his eyes.

The smell of face-powder hung in the air.

'Smells like a bloody ladies' boudoir!' He heard Bill Olsen's sardonic voice in his imagination. Memories of the hunting expeditions in the sunlit garden and the evenings by the fire on the threshold of the Kremlin chamber floated through his mind.

They crossed the Channel and at midnight they came into Dover. Dilke listened to the man and the woman talking; they were tired and they agreed that as the office would not be open till nine thirty there was no reason to drive straight to London. They rode through Dover and pulled into the first lay-by on the A.2.

Dilke lay and watched the agents reflected in the mirror over his head; the woman curled up in the back and the man dozed in the front.

Dilke closed his eyes again.

The sun had gone out of his memories; they were now sombre; he reviewed once more the worn movie of the night on Volsk's head. The car rocked in the turbulent air waves left by passing container trucks . . . a patrol car

wailed past, the revolving bowl on its roof throwing a
flashing corpse-blue light on the side of the sleeping
agent's face . . . a rainstorm drifted in from the Channel,
whispering across the countryside, drumming on the roof
of the car, trickling in jerking blobs down the car windows . . .

Dilke slept and had a dream.

He dreamt that he was at the Kremlin. In place of the
sliding brass door covering the entrance to the lock were
two glass slides. He was imprisoned between them; far
below on the foot of the shed he could see a tiny figure;
he watched it, his heart thudding with apprehension. It
began to grow in size as if exploding from within; it
grew into a monstrous naked figure, superbly muscled; on
the column of its neck was a wolf's head. The head revolved on the neck; a light behind the blue eyes flashed
on and off as the head spun slowly round; from its jaws
came a fluctuating howl. The monster's fingers pressed a
doll-like figure to its chest; Dilke's eyes widened. It was
Hyacinthe. She faced Dilke; her legs and feet together, her
arms raised stiffly sideways, her palms towards him. His
eyes were fixed on her trancelike face; the eyes were shut,
and slowly, a tear of blood welled up beneath each
lowered lid. The drops grew in size then rolled over the
curve of her cheeks and splashed down on to the fingers
of the huge hands.

Dilke was crushed tight between the walls of glass, held
in the same crucified position as the girl; he could not
move; he could not call out. A scream of rage and horror
was locked inside him, the glass pressed against his burst-
ing lungs, the heavy beat in his breast slowed . . . his
heart stopped . . .

He woke, his body rigid, his stiff arms propping him
up, his head thrown back between his shoulder blades, his
voice choked in his throat as if by a gag. Then he fell
back on the bed with a groan.

The rain had stopped and the moon shone full into
the great oyster shell of the compact.

He heard a low voice beside him; Hyacinthe lay curled
like a black cat a little distance away. Her eyes were
closed, her lips trembled in a smile, her hand reached out
as if to touch someone. *'Father?'* she murmured.

He fell asleep, sinking down through layers of sadness and futility.

At five the man yawned prodigiously, got out of the car to massage the stiffness out of his limbs and then started the last lap to London.

At nine he acknowledged the salute of the Ministry car park attendant, cut the engine, reached out and snapped shut the lid of the compact and carried it, cradled in his hand, in the pocket of his sports jacket. The darkness inside the compact was total, the cloying scent of face-powder suffocating. By their movements Dilke could trace their progress along the familiar corridors and up the stairs to his old office. The heat from the agent's hand penetrated the walls of the compact till it was as hot as the anteroom to a sauna bath.

They heard a click as the compact was put down on a desk top. A muffled sound of dialling was followed by the indistinct voice of the agent. A cupboard door was opened and shut, there was a thud as a heavy object was put down on the desk beside them, then the lid swung open and a blaze of light fell on them.

'Major Price says you are to ring him at nine thirty.'

Dilke stood up in the middle of the puff and watched the receding head and shoulders of the man vanish below the rim of the compact. The door opened and the pneumatic door-shutter gave a long asthmatic wheeze, they heard footsteps on the corridor lino and the clicking of heels descending the stone stairs. Dilke tipped a hand at the closed door, 'And he didn't even say goodbye!'

Hyacinthe smiled uncertainly.

They waded laboriously to the edge of the powder puff and looked over the rim of the compact. Before them was the spherical gyro-transporter. They entered it and found the radio phone on the couch where Dilke had left it. The wheel above them was motionless. Dilke lay on the couch and looked up at it, its silence and weight seemed to menace him. His depression deepened as he tried to rehearse in his mind what he was going to say.

The plain fact was that the mission had failed and he faced a possible interview with Lord Raglen with dread.

Hyacinthe sat for a while on the couch, then, like a

bored child, she walked slowly round the perimeter of
the chamber, gazed wonderingly up at the gyro-wheel and
delicately touched the smooth surface of its central column
with her fingertips.

The radio phone buzzed before Dilke could ring Price.
Price was at his most businesslike and cryptic, he wanted
a report quickly to show to Lord Raglen, he told Dilke
that he was taping their conversation and asked him to
give a detailed verbal account of the mission immediately.
Dilke described the events in Rumania from the moment
he was put down on the Arad to Bucharest road until he
was picked up almost a week later. He included everything which he thought relevant, leaving out no facts, but
omitting personal comments. He finished in a flat, subdued voice; 'I regret to say so, Major Price, but in effect
the mission has been a failure. I especially regret the
deaths of Olsen and Scott-Milne, and I wish to register
the fact that they share no blame for the lack of success.'

His speech had become starched with the sort of
officialese which he abhorred—he thought sourly that the
words could have come from the mouth of Major Price
himself.

'Thank you, Captain Dilke. Lord Raglen is returning
from Scotland tonight and may wish to see you.'

Dilke put down the radio, folded his arms and gazed
listlessly at his pencil-thin reflection in the shining gyroscope spindle.

'What will happen now, Mathew?'

Hyacinthe's timid question interrupted his thoughts.
Without answering he picked up the handpiece and dialled
Price.

'Major Price, can you arrange for me to have clothing
for Miss Kasama and myself? If we are to stay here tonight it will be cold. In fact I'd be glad if you could let
us have blankets too . . . We will need something to eat,
please; we left our food in the tin box in which your
agents brought us back from Rumania. There is also a
map case in the box with a roll of film in it which you
might like to have—the box is probably still in the car.'

'I'll see what I can do, Captain. I'll have some things
left at your transporter entrance this afternoon.'

A ration pack and a blanket each were delivered as

Price had promised. The thin padding on the couch made a hard bed after the powder puff. Dilke lay on the cold bench, an arm across his face, shielding his eyes from the bare bulb high in the roof of the sphere.

The effort of recollection which he had made in order to give his report had sharpened his memories and he brooded over them. Though he could see no way in which he could have prevented the disaster, the knowledge that the consequences might endanger the miniaturization programme filled him with despondency. The work of chemists, engineers and mathematicians; the sacrifices of the men in the chain of miniaturization; the deaths of Henry and Bill Olsen . . . And—he recognized self-interest—what would happen to a failed micro-spy?

4

In the morning, and without warning, the sphere lurched and became airborne. In a little while it landed and the radio phone said, 'Price here. Lord Raglen is waiting, please step outside.'

It was like all his interviews with headmasters, appointments boards and disciplinary committees rolled into one.

As he walked down the ramp on to Lord Raglen's desk he became aware of a scratchy voice talking against a hissing background.

'. . . in effect the mission has been a failure. I especially regret the deaths of Olsen and Scott-Milne and I wish to register the fact that they share no blame for the lack of success.'

The hiss went evenly on; Dilke looked up at the huge

revolving spools and the belt of tape which moved between them; Raglen's white hand reached out and stabbed the recorder's 'stop' button. There was silence broken only by the heavy tick of a Big Ben wrist-watch.

Today's blotting paper colour was tan. Today, Dilke was not in the Siberian glare of a prison camp desk light; the blotting-pad on which he walked was lit by the late September sun. The hand knocked down a lever on the intercom—'Price, I want you to listen to this. Where is Dilke? Is he here?' The great face bent over the pad, the jowls swelling over the high white collar. 'All right, all right, I can see him.' The massive torso straightened, the head receded, the hand rested on the desk on each side of the brown carpet on which Dilke stood.

'Captain Dilke.' There was a long House-of-Lords' pause.

'Captain Dilke. I have listened to the report on your Balkan trip. It is true that you did not achieve the object of your mission—and to this extent it has been a failure. You have, however, returned with a deal of information about the state of Communist miniaturization which this department finds valuable. Moreover, by killing the man Batzar you may have held up their programme. Batzar, we have discovered, was not merely a counter-agent but had a considerable scientific reputation and it is possible that he was in charge of their miniaturizing programme.'

Dilke was dazed, he could not yet grasp the implications of Lord Raglen's words.

'But you have, in fact, returned with something which I value even more than the successful accomplishment of your given mission . . .'

Dilke stared up; the god-head smiled distantly.

'. . . the film with which you returned has given us information of a particularly valuable nature.' The soft hand passed over Dilke's head and lifted from the desk a black-and-white photograph. It held the huge print curved between finger and thumb for Dilke to see; the sun made a streak of reflected light down its glossy surface and the grain was as big as bricks—but Dilke recognized the marble top, the hand with the Cuban cigar, the battered steel box and the papers within it.

'What you have brought to us, Captain, is a military

code now used extensively in Russia and the Balkans. It has enabled us to decipher much material which we already held . . . and there is no reason why it should be changed yet.

'You gave us thirty-six excellent pictures of it—it was in the dispatch box lid.'

Dilke had come before Jehovah to be destroyed by words.

Now Raglen's approbation transported him from a mood of apprehension to one of flushed elation. He glanced back at Hyacinthe but she had remained in the shadow of the transporter.

'We will continue with miniaturization. You have headed the pilot scheme and I want you to control the next phase; Major Price has the details.'

Lord Raglen's hands came together on the blotter six inches from Dilke. His moon face loomed above the massive interlaced fingers. For a moment the eyes gazed across the room, then they returned to the tiny figure on the tan paper.

'I wish to take this opportunity, Captain, to express my regret that no official recognition can be made . . .' he cleared his throat . . . 'please accept my sympathy for the loss of your men.'

The awkward phrases offering condolence gave a new turn to Dilke's emotions; he gazed up into the pale eyes and swallowed hard. The interlocked fingers parted, a hand reached out and cut off Price on the intercom: the interview was finished.

5

Dilke yawned, cupped a hand across his face and squeezed hard. The wide table at which he sat was littered with papers and box files. He raised the mug which had been placed at his elbow and sipped hot coffee.

From the minature pre-fab which rested on the window ledge of his old office he looked out on St. James's Park.

It was after seven. The ranks of civil service cars had left the car park, queued to cross Westminster Bridge and dispersed to the southern suburbs. The side lights of a cab travelling towards the Mall moved beneath the trees which shadowed the road. The dim flash of a wing marked the island where the park pelicans were settling for the night.

For a fortnight he had worked with Price on the plan for a micro-community; the plan had already existed in outline but not in detail. A corps of a hundred micro-men was to be trained in a six month's period. Dilke had picked ten key men from the file of volunteers, to train as instructors to the remainder.

He had ordered stores and equipment and had checked the typescript of his survival manual.

He would continue to use his garden and the allotment as a training ground and men and equipment would be delivered directly to the base of the old shed—Lord Raglen had relented and raised the absolute secrecy on the Kremlin. His preparations were finished: tomorrow he would arrange transport.

Above the trees a geometric pattern of lights built up on the dark rectangle of the Hilton.

A jet whistled hoarsely overhead.

Dilke became aware of the silence within the room. He turned and looked at Hyacinthe.

She lay back on the divan in the fading light, a cup between her hands, gazing past him at the sky. Her expression was pensive—almost melancholy.

The jet dropped a wing and slanted off towards London Airport, sailing down the sky into the dirty pink band of air which submerged Hammersmith. Her eyes followed its blinking wing lights: red, green—red, green—red, green . . .

Dilke suddenly realized that the affection which had grown between them had faded. His preoccupation with planning had turned his thoughts inwards; for days he had hardly spoken to her and his taciturnity had driven her back into silence.

'Hyacinthe.'

His low voice roused her from her reverie.

'Mathew?'

'Tomorrow I must go into the country.'

She remained silent.

'If you wish, you can stay behind. You could help by checking stores through and that sort of thing, but . . .' he hesitated . . . 'I would like you to come with me.'

The room was almost dark, he could not see her face. 'It will be hard to begin with. But I will have to set up an office at the base camp and you could run it . . .'

She smiled in the darkness, 'And teach you all Political Science?'

On an impulse Dilke arranged to be dropped at the window seat and not at the shed.

Dust lay thick on the mesh of spider's webs in the window and covered the packing case which stood at the centre of the seat. Dilke ran his hand across the half-obscured lettering: THIS WAY UP—Charlie never did get his motor.

They left the house, climbed the rockery and walked along the disused ant track. Haze obscured the bright autumn sun, filling the familiar landscape with soft light.

As they passed beneath the dying hollyhocks and travelled across the plains and through the plantation,

Dilke's mood was buoyant. Hyacinthe smiled at his air of proprietorship but was a little alarmed by his description of the hazards which he had met when he was first a micro-man.

At the end of the day they descended the last slope and stood before the huge shed.

An agent had leased the allotment and removed the boards which had been nailed across the door; a heavy new padlock secured it.

They climbed the threshold and walked under the door. A neat civil service hand had been at work; the box had been lifted from the sacking in the corner and set down in the middle of the hut.

Dilke's eyes travelled up the grey façade to the platform.

Bill Olsen's trophies still hung above the sliding door, its brass surface was blackened by smoke from the fires which had burned on the ledge. A hole cut in the back of the lock would give access to the interior of the box. He would have floors put in . . . a lift installed . . . dormitories, dining halls, kitchens . . . an armoury, a laboratory, a gymnasium . . .

The light was fading perceptibly, the October wind hit the cliff face of the hut and moaned under the door; suddenly it felt cold; he pulled the collar of his padded grey jacket up round his ears and thrust his hands into its deep pockets. Outside, the wind hustled yellowing leaves against the side of the hut. A single dead leaf was blown under the door and cartwheeled slowly past the two tiny figures.

Dilke felt a cold hand slip into his pocket; their palms came together, their fingers interwined; they walked towards the box, following the spinning leaf down the long perspective of planks.

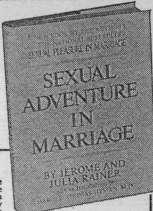

For the Sunday cyclist... for the cross-country tourist... whether you ride for better health, for sport, or for the sheer fun of it,

GET
THE COMPLETE BOOK OF BICYCLING

The First Comprehensive Guide To All Aspects of Bicycles and Bicycling

JUST A FEW OF THE HUNDREDS OF EXCITING TIPS YOU'LL FIND:

- A simple way to increase your cycling efficiency by 30 to 40%—breeze over hilltops while others are struggling behind.
- 13 special safety tips for youngsters.
- How to read a bicycle's specifications to know if you're getting a superior one or a dud.
- How to know whether to buy a 3-speed to start with, or a 10-speed.
- How to select the right kind of equipment for touring or camping.
- How to minimize danger when cycling in the city.

▼ AT YOUR BOOKSTORE OR MAIL THIS COUPON NOW FOR FREE 30-DAY TRIAL ▼

C4/1